T0063105

"THE CROW'S CRY 2"

Anastasia Shmaryan

Trafford PUBLISHING® www.trafford.com
North America & international
toll-free: 1 888 232 4444 (USA & Canada)
fax: 812 355 4082

PART I

CHAPTER 1

It's time on the verge of midnight at the Great Lakes. Where came into view two men, who are Robert Lipinski and Dan Ming sit in the interior of a van that on fire, as it's at brink of bursting.

On the spot Dan has unlocked the back car window, as both at once were out, and about of a flamed truck. Next saw flames from a blast spew into the air, as a thunderous echo is heard around. After a van fell into the water, and has exploded. Flashes of light in blitz, at the same time aside a blast trails, then spits, as it's evaporating into a haze.

While a magpie is soaring in mid-air, and began crying out; where its resonance heard far and wide.

. . . So far the two have survived an awful explosion. Given that all around be ruins, and are smelt from a blaze in the air. This has spread far and wide.

In split seconds, miraculously from under the water up on the surface, are having flown up two men's head.

Before now it had passed mid-night at The Great Lakes, where saw Robert Lipinski swam in front of Dan Ming. Since the duo heads swam from under water, where are both appearing up on the surface of a stream? On a whim Robert stops, but is wheezing; next he looks around, and anxiously orders Dan to: 'Dan, we must do a quick swim, and try to get lost in the water, before foggy disappears?'—

At a critical point Rob Lipinski with Dan Ming are begun swimming away; and being in the direction of the border with Canada.

Later that night, saw this duo is still swam in the Lakes, whilst being in the water for relatively of time.

A sudden current began suffocating by stream, while those two are going for a dip swim . . .

When Dan next looks around, and has become scared; but he is also out of breath: 'Rob, Goddamn . . . !'—Dan stops for a second, as if takes in what he has said. He then briefly revised himself: 'Wally, is you accepting as true that we can make it?'—Seen Rob is shaken his head, as if agreed. Effect of being long in the water made its toll upon them: Rob is out of breath. Yet, by spattering out the water he nods, and is affirmed: 'Yeah! Maybe! Hold on pal! It is awful, what we have gone through! And, how much is ahead for us to be taken, my friend?'—As Dan moves his head up and down: 'True! Let us hope for the best? Ah! Oh . . .'—Rob is panting, but nods with his head, and gave a purpose: 'We must pray! Ah! It's rough water here. Ah, oh . . .'—Robert and Dan are thinking for a bit.

After seeing both as one are going for a dip swim . . .

Robert has first disappeared deep into the water; following him is Dan. Just as they are swimming, there having seen boundless, where both surrounded by coldness of stream, for relatively of time . . .

To some degree those two wind up, as are realizing they should swim first to Green Bay, Wisconsin.

A bit later, those two peek the shore in a close proximity to their respite, while they are looking at each other with shared view.

In a difficult situation they have made an effort, when are begun swimming in double time, in an attempt to seek refuge somewhere . . .

CHAPTER 2

In next to no time this double act is out of the water, and where they debark onto a dry land.

Once they look around, in an effort to find safe haven, as well to dry up on that site . . . When Robert next looks closely over yonder, he has spotted a group of fishermen. A sudden he tags Dan's on sleeve, like an idea came to his mind. Ensuing Robert angles his head, and points to them:

'Dan, do you see those fishermen, over there?'—

Dan saw an opportunity; and goes around, is looking to the side of, where the men stood. He turns back, and says-so: 'Yeah! But my question is, what you intend to do about it?'—

Robert momentarily is thinking for a minute . . .

A sudden certain idea hits him; and Rob is alleged:

'Do you think, what I am thinking, Dan?'—

On a critical point, Robert puts one free hand into his pocket, and inserts from a wrapped bag. After he raises his head up, leans down, and gave a hint by winking to those men. Next he points to a heap that is hidden in his wet pants: 'We need to go, and negotiate with those fishermen, in a flash, Dan?'—

Now Robert comes back with a solution, it seems that something sink to him. He winks, and adroitly gave hints: 'I know what to do! Dan, let's go with to negotiate with those fishermen! They will help us, I bet on that?'—Robert is hesitant; and at last, he leans down, and points to his pocket, where has apparently carried in a tiny bag all along, from the time when the blasts struck. Thus both have left.

Thence Robert and Dan are accepted wisdom . . .

Later that night, in a refuge shack look-see is a group of fishermen that seated around. Whereas on other side of the roomy seen Robert, who has rested in a chair, and seated alongside him is Dan.

Ensuing Rob starts having a friendly chat with the fishermen: 'Dudes, let's be in agreement to budge us in one of your boats? You will be profiting from crossing to Canada! In a current weather, is no-win situation for fishing anyway? Oh, come on let us make a deal, friends . . .'—

Seen Robert sits beside fishermen, who are amused, and hearing those myths to be told amid them.

At that crucial moment, in the twinkling of an eye both parties are having agreed.

At the same night, approximately 3 a.m. Robert gets aboard one of the fishermen boat. There he is lying down on bottom of the vessel. Given that Dan too is following him behind.

Being on board Dan doesn't bend down. On that incident Rob whispers, but is edgy: 'What in Hell are you doing, man? Get down! Before Cops find us here?'—On the spot, Robert clues Dan up: 'Get down, Dan, and cover your head?'—Clumsily Dan bows his head down: 'I am sorry, pal! I didn't think straight!'—In that case Robert provides Dan with a throw so that his pal covers himself over: 'All right! Calm down, pal, and put your head down? But Dan, cover yourself with only half of quilt?'—

With a delay, Rob turns aside, and raises head up to face fishermen; next he orders them: 'Dudes, let's cast off! Seven feet to us under the kills!'—

By way of his head bobs down, and he saw to Dan with a wink.

At some stage of waiting to cast off, Dan is tense, impassive, but he's nosey: 'Rob, what will happen to us?'—Rob has taken gulp of air; but he looks lost, and it's safe for guesswork. Apparently he is pursuing horizon overhead: 'I don't know, Dan? We must reach Canada first. Once from there we will see, what may turn out for us?'—

In next to no time view of a fishing boat cast off accompanied by the double act that, being aboard.

Before long this boat has disappeared into a mist . . .

CHAPTER 3

A t the same morning, meanwhile in the Lipinski house saw Rosalyn, who is half-asleep, when walking in the family room. Here, as usual she switches on television; is made herself comfortable, takes the weight off her foot to relax on sofa, beside Hugo.

A sudden broadcast is started, where Robert's photo has shown along with a young Chinese man, while the reportage being on the air. Rosalyn is watching the photographs on TV in panic. Like so she has become sadden when saw; as is heard the reporter put in the picture that, be aired on TV: "Here some breaking news!"—This news reader stops for a bit, and is ongoing: "Photo of two criminals be shown on TV, had driven away in a van, when attempted to flee the police! In effort to catch them, the police opened fire on their van! Unfortunately the double act's truck hit bridge's fences that, it has plunged into the Lake . . . It has resulted of accident on the scene, as the van burst in flames! The two presumably died, caused by frosty temperature and chilly waters!"—The newsreader stops; inhales, and is enduring: "Police is identified those suspects. "Their names are Robert Lipinski and Dan Ming! Due to search for them, is ongoing . . ."—This reporter protracts with news, as his voice perceive sound, but it's not be heard by Rosalyn.

Look-see Rosalyn has turned pale, equally being her expression of grief. Hugo sits near her side, and hugs her, but has struggled calming his wife down, who is hysterical? To evaluate, her condition being close to unconsciousness . . .

. . . Over time Rosalyn is subsided; then she told her husband, still being distressed to cry: 'Oh, dear Lord! He is my son, Robert! How such a horror happened? What has my son done wrong? This couldn't be true? Why, God?'—Hugo still holds Rosalyn in his arms, so as to calm her down. He talks, be composed: 'So-so! There you're. I don't trust them! What Rob isn't alive? It's not real! Rosy, the police have made it up!'—

CHAPTER 4

It's a vision of bluish-purple crack of dawn outskirts of Canada, with a frosty weather there.

At the present see Robert and Dan are moved on the picked up car, just as they progressing with care . . .

A minute ago Robert and Dan have exited off picked up motor vehicle; and now they are on course for . . .

Later that morning in Canada environs, see they are under your own steaming, relatively a few miles . . .

Time in between, on a transitory traffic lane this duo make a left turn. Saw both is kept walking; when next they are begun moving uphill.

By next travel they are begun climbing up on top of the mounts peaks.

Once getting up to the top, they have reached the first goal. Next both are begun descending down the mountains as one . . .

Still this duo on foot for a relatively few miles, except both are free of talking. At that juncture Rob breaks a madcap peace, what it's be suspected; thus he talks urgently: 'Listen, Dan, forget my real name don't call me Rob, okay? Try getting used to me, as Wally Miser, pal, are we decided on?'—Dan looks at Robert, and shakes his head, when he is reacting: 'Rob, I just think, how we were able to escape those bloody Cops?'—Except Rob, who is appeared worried, for ducks his head, like he's decided: 'Yeah in true-life sometimes it happens?'—Robert stops; takes breathes; and prolongs, be sad: 'I am agonizing that Cyclops has got Nora? He can imperil her . . . ?'—But Dan breaks in, it's seeming is nosy: 'What in hell, he wants from her?'—Dan stops short; thinks for a bit; as if something sinks to him: 'What if Cyclops tries Nora? Now you far-off from her, but he will take advantage, so as to have her? He can press on Nora, no matter what it takes? And, she will give in, at last into Cyclops demands?'—Now Robert is thinking silently. Hearing as he began talking, is gloomy: 'I don't think it will happen, because Nora hates Cyclops guts! How this Son of a Bitch found out about our intents?'—Resultant, Dan spins to express his opinion, like he is in no doubts:

'I am sure Cyclops was spying on us?'—

Like so, they are accepted wisdom.

At some stage of climbing, this duo look-see a ranch at borders, outskirts of Canada. Hot on the heel they are resulting: and having gone in hub, far-off the US. It's a victory for them.

Later that morning they are spotting and Auto shop'; where put up for sale having contained of scooters, so as to profit from other motor vehicles in there. Naturally Rob speaks up his mind, and is cunning: 'How about you and me borrow a scooter from this shop that have got too many over there, my friend?'— Though both are obviously scared; still Dan swivels to scrutiny the site. He then mumbles, as if he is tense: 'Are you crazy? What if a siren catches us? Just look inside? There is no way . . .'—

Despite those two have disagreed; eventually both are breaking into an Auto-shop without hesitation.

Now view this duo is riding aboard scooter on full-speed. Seen the two are wearing dark leather outfit on that, covers in gears from their tip to toes.

Before long, the rider a fast get-up-and-go on the scooter, as those forcing via into divided highway.

Eventually those riders are rotating that, made the way through on a scooter and moved up to the signs.

By daytime the duo is riding on the scooter along the highway, on a full-speed.

By their next travel views the riders are forcing in speedily to limited-access highway on a scooter.

At length the riders are rotating scooter, having made their way through to the signs. A sudden Dan brings to a halt scooter, before the signs emerge; then their head up > The Airport > City Center . . .

Dan raises a hand up to show on the signs: 'Rob!'—

He stops short; briefly became silent; by his expression tells he's remembered something. Dan is shaken his head; spits aside; he says of regret: 'Damn! Wally, you see signs over there?'—Robert nods his head up and down, it's seeming is certain: 'Yeah! We are on the right track!'—

Dan turns his head around; then leans his upper-body to point of a poster that, mysteriously hanging; and shows it to Rob: 'Do you see a poster whine for the Circus?'—Rob is assuming all, appears lost at sea: 'Yeah! What do you have in mind?'—In a critical point Dan talks with confidence: 'I have a strategy! And we have to stick to it? Let's go, Wally, I will tell on the way!'—Robert leans toward Dan, who is prying: 'Oh come on, Dan! Tell me, now?'—

Dan meanwhile, curves to start on scooter's speed, and nods his head: 'Okeydokey! We can go for magic transformation? What do you think?'—Given Dan looks be dazed that, stumbled: 'Well, for myself . . .'—Rob prevents him from talking, and alone is declared: 'Let's hurry up, then?'—

CHAPTER 5

For now it's mauve crack of dawn, outskirts of the US. At this point attracts the attention Eleanor, who's asleep in the secured room, and being lying under the bed-covers?

A sudden access gets wide-open, where on doorsteps came into view inspector Colubrine: a walk in; near him is Martin-Cyclops that, held breakfast set for one on a tray in his hands. The men have worn suits, and both being mysterious. Martin is in motion, when he puts a tray down on the table. In there is not seen a single window.

Now Martin turns aside, in a flash, and began talking to Nora, be joyful: 'Good morning, runaway bride? How did you sleep, Nora? I hope well . . . ?'—

Nora contrary looks at those two, as goes in with abhorrence; is ironic, as tackles them: 'Thanks to your prayers, I am fine!'— Those men look at each other, are raising their browse up. Despite Colubrine is begun talking calmly: 'Why are you cynical, Miss Lonsdale? Martin has saved your life then and there?'—As Martin's heard the remarks, he became blissful. On a whim he points his hand to a tray, and alone is declared: 'I have brought you breakfast? Come on get up, Eleanor, and have something to eat?'—Still Nora doesn't get up of bed; hearing her tongue in cheek, and it is shaken her head: 'No, thanks! I am afraid that meal would-be stuck in my throat!'—But her suchlike talk doesn't bother Martin, who is cool and certain: 'Why are you hostile toward me? I came with good deeds to you, Nora!'—On a whim Eleanor irked with harsh words: 'Why wouldn't I? Don't pull my leg! I am aware of you're good deeds, Martin!'—At this time Colubrine disrupts her; and alone make-believe Nora, as he speaks firmly: 'That's enough! Mrs. Lipinski . . .'—He then stops; it seem he wants to confirm with Nora on her marital status: 'Are you really married to Lipinski?'—Nora nods with her head up and down, looks as if her is proud of it, which she's confirmed: 'Yes! My name is Mrs. Lipinski, without a doubt!'—

Colubrine on a critical point folds a hand upon his chest, to give her an idea about him being sorrow. His endorsement is so as to trick her in: 'You need to know madam that, we are sorry for the loss of your husband . . .'—Barring Nora cuts him short that, says in quirk of fate: 'Do you really? I can hardly believe it!'—A Chief became annoyed, and responds firm: 'You have to be gracious with us! Because we have proof that you were involved odds-on in all, thus you can end up in jail, instead of your late husband? We have made the Law here, and you must abide by it!'—Now Eleanor still lies in bed; but turns pale, as a result she began yelling, is jumpy: 'Then, I want to leave, let me go? If not, I demand a Defense Lawyer, and a fair trial!'—After hearing Nora's accusations, inspector appears is displeased. As be wise Colubrine, without more ado, began exiting the secret room? Before Colubrine exits, Martin spins see to the Chief, while inclines like wants handle solo, what is arisen with her?

Once inspector has left, Martin next turns back facing Eleanor, he seems is keen; and is murmuring:

'Significantly that last night you were caught crossing the border? Secondly, you owe us being alive, Nora, otherwise you would-be dead before now, in that burned van with them, on the Lakes . . .'—

Eleanor stops him, seen her be furious: 'It's your entire fault! If you're people have not chased after Robert and Dan's van, the blasts would not strike?'—Impulsively Martin raises head up; looks at her ardently, and he is declared: 'Nora, you're an amazing woman!'—He is reaching hand to her, while she has tried to shy away; his hand stretchy, it seems adores her that, he is begging: 'Nora, you're worthy for a better live, then live with a thief . . .'—But Nora prevents him of talking; and without ado stars a spat, as she is gnashing her teeth: 'You don't have moral right to mess around in my 'personal live with Robert, my husband! And your rotten words in his memory it's cruel!'— Nora began sobbing. Yet, Martin is breathless; as folds up his hands, seem is begging her to love him, ardently: 'I love you, Nora! I 'would do anything to make you happy! If you only give me a chance to prove it . . . ?'—On a critical point Nora prevents him from saying more; himself tells with grim looks: 'If Robert did really die in the explosion? I will 'never forgive you for that, firstly! Secondly, Rob was a fine and kind man . . .'— Martin instead, roars out of jealousy: 'Yea, a fine criminal! He had caused a man to become crippled! Most importantly, he has mixed up my life . . .'—On a whim Nora stops him; says by fret: 'Back then it was an accident! But if you tried talk crap to me, without any respect for Rob's death! Then, I ask you to leave right now, Martin!'—Unwisely, he became heated, and yet: 'You said he was gallant! Well, Rob has left you, Nora? While alone he is escaped abroad?'—In a flash Nora's eyes began glowing; she is eager, as trying to find more about it. Nora takes in: 'What have you said a minute ago? My Rob is alive? Thank you, God!'—She skews, and is asking him:' Where is my husband? I want to 'see him?'—

On the spot her voice altered to angry: 'Though Martin, you let the police shoot at him? You have allowed his van to blow up!'—On a whim she stops; and is telling more: 'And, why should Rob go to jail, just to oblige you? Then why your people have brought me in here?'—Instinctively Nora prevents him from what's been unsaid. For rather unforeseen hits her: 'Aha! I get it! You detained me, so as to entice Robert for . . . ?"—Here Martin gave a smirk, as his shoulders are shaken. His expression is shown of a madman; when he reacts by way of irony or fret: 'Well well, Nora you're spot-on! Congrats! But we will catch him, if he is alive? When Robert, dearest shows up, I will make sure that, he is sent directly to jail! And, Justice will be served!'—

Spontaneous Nora jumps up of bed, holds a knuckle ahead to fight. Resultant Nora kicks Martin in the crouch; laid-backs, and yells; her voice is edgy:

'You don't have guts for? Don't you dare come near me? You will pay dearly for it, Cyclops!'—

CHAPTER 6

Here opens a view of a lovely sunrise in Canada, where in close proximity to other side of the border, be set tent.

There saw Robert, who is walking beside Dan?

Both has resultant, and entered premises of the Circus. The Display come into sight from all sides', where entry to be ready every minute welcomes to perform in the Show, on these large-scale acts of the Circus, and throughout the duo's routines.

This duo peeks collection of imitation apparatus. One of those fascinating superstars, are privileged to attract crowds who come to see, which act is delivered amazing in the Show under a grand tent, by performing tricks?

Ten minutes later in an office of the Circus sees a man in his late forties, who name is Wallace Summer that be seated around the desk. On opposite side is seen Rob called Wally, who stood in front of Dan; but he gets ready to leave. Given that this duo is in deep discussion between each other.

A bit later Wallace watches Robert be called Wally and Dan's in performance:

'What are your names, gentlemen?'—Robert is hesitant, as begun talking: 'I am Ro . . . I mean Wally Miser!'—Dan jumps in the midst of introducing himself: 'And my name Sang, sir!'— Summer looks at the two, is thinking in silence: 'So, gentlemen, what exotic you two are capable of, performing in our Circus?'— Robert looks at Dan awkwardly; both seem being scared stiff. Robert then invites: 'Sir, I don't understand you?'—Wallace at that moment, bows head down, like is in search of something. He has risen up; backs his head to face this duo, while held a poster in his hand; he then is given it to them: 'Guys, do you see this poster? Our show is called "The Earth Finest Circus"?'—

Now Wallace points his hand to a Poster: 'Herein the artists are performing at Circus super-duper, exclusively with the animals. Like this, and more of magical Tricks!'—The duo glances meticulously on a poster; at some stage of silent, they are making gestures with mimics to one another. Time in between, Wallace declares: 'Our Show was reincarnated from the time, when we had problems then and there with that franchise.'—Now it's apparent struck Rob: 'Sir, my friend and I are desperate to get an opening and working in this circus?'—Being cunning Robert too tries to fill a gap without avoiding suspicion; it is resulting he asks Wallace over: 'Sir, you said reincarnation . . .'—On a whim Wallace disrupts Rob, like is intrigued by his query: 'I don't know, what the hell you are talking about? Just tell me if the two of you know how to bring in my circus some new tricks as to perform?'—On the spot Dan intrudes: 'Sir, my partner and I are glad bringing in the circus: "A Double Act" featuring a magpie: this bird will be the real Star of our act, and in your Circus!'—

Now, Wallace is thinking a bit: 'Really? This sounds exciting! Where is your bird? I feel like to view it, what you can do in the company of a crow? That's what you have said?'—But Rob corrects him:

'No it's a magpie, sir!'—Rob immediately starts to reflecting on the lot: 'Not any birds, but a well 'trained one! For my part I can perform as a flying acrobat, together with my magpie?'—Seen Wallace leers, but his body is shaken: 'Okay! But have you ever flew on trapeze?'—Robert observes Wallace; at the same time as be lost; he then shaken his head. Yet, Robert rejoins: 'No!'—

It's like a sudden idea is mind-stricken him:' But, I can invent some Magic scenes?'—

CHAPTER 7

Its nightfall in US, where outer reaches came into the sight a location, to where a chain of vehicles has arrived.

Next the cars have stopped all at once, near the entrance of a grand building; there saw one of these car's door that has dark glass-sills, get unlocked.

From there a few folks are getting out of cars, amid which sees are: Hugo and Rosalyn. This pair stood and is looking round; both are scared stiff . . .

From nowhere Martin emerges, be keen: 'Hey, you're two, let us moving along?'—

This duo awkwardly is looking at each-other, in silence. Seen Hugo slants toward his wife; and signs with his eyes; he then murmurs: 'Rosy, try not to give in?'—Rosalyn is upset, and curves closer to him, mumbling: 'How?'—And Hugo points out: 'For your son's sake, Rosy, Okay?'—Rosalyn barely nods her head, and takes a lungful of air.

At that juncture some of the police began forcing those two to move ahead . . .

Later that night, in premises, in hidden room that gave the impression of is an interrogation area. Here be seated Hugo at the table; seen he is tied up to a chair. At sideward saw inspector Colubrine be attentive. Around the place light is blurry.

For the time being, behind the mirror walls Martin is stood alongside another officer, and he seems being edgy, but desperate.

Briefly in interrogation room Hugo looks around the roomy, and he is dispirited; but confident.

At this time Colubrine began talking: 'Mister Morales, do know why you were brought in here?'—

At this instant is silence. As Hugo turns his head back, is facing Colubrine who is shaken with his neck up and down.

Then Hugo breaks a dead silence: 'No! But I want know, where is my wife?'—Seen this inspector acts in response: 'You will, Hugo, soon enough!'—Next the inspector is placed a hand on the table.

Meanwhile, peace remains during cross-examination; resulting Colubrine informs Hugo: 'Not, until you tell me, where is your Step-son Robert Lipinski?'—

Saw Hugo is paying special attention to the inspector's eyes, as if something sinks to him; in that case he smirks, but wouldn't move by an inch. Hugo acts in respond: 'Considering tragedy that has happened to Robert and his friend, it without doubt, was provoked by your people, inspector!'—Be in a difficult situation, Hugo continued: 'What make sense to me, inspector . . .'—It's like as if Hugo has read-through his mind. Inspector shakes his head. Be seated, on a critical point Hugo gave his opinion: '. . . is that your people are still searching for Robert? But, in vein, he is nowhere to be found? True or not, inspector?'—

Period in-between, behind the mirror walls, Martin is impatient, when raised his hands up 'like a cat on a hot tin roof', and he implies: 'Hugo is deceiving us, as this bastard knew something?'—

Back in the interrogation room sees the inspector, shakes his head is, as appears gloomy, but remained cool: 'Mister Morales, young Lipinski was not your son! So, it's in your best interest to tell us now, whereabouts he is?'—Hugo sneers: 'Even if I knew, I wouldn't tell you! . . .'—He inhales, and is cocky.

Meanwhile, behind mirror walls Martin is raring to go, when in discussion with one from the forces:

'Look at him, he is cocky, and a liar?'—Given that officer spanks Martin over his upper arms:

'Oh come on, McDermott, be cool! Give the Chief some time?'—Here Martin is frantic: 'But I won't wait long? I will beat the shit out of him to reveal, where young Lipinski is?'—

Backside in the interrogating room a crack in that case, though Hugo gave the lowdown: '. . . do you know, why, inspector? Because your people hunting him like he is a monster! But you know something, you are wrong, Robert is a good, and kind man!'—

Colubrine analyses a bit; and swing with his upper arm, it seems is decisive: 'Mister Morales, have you ever come across of good Cops and bad Cop?'—But Hugo is tongue-tied, looks at him and puzzled: 'It doesn't sink to me what you meant, inspector?'— In that case Colubrine smirks: 'Hugo, let me explain to you. I am a good Cop, but if you refuse to tell us, what you know of young Lipinski's dealing? You will find out!'—Colubrine stops; coughs up, while he stood by way of rotating and is facing the mirror wall. Next he gave a nod to someone behind glass: likely to go ahead for an important person? As Colubrine has resulted; and turned back to face Hugo; he speaks up his mind: 'Well, in that case you don't leave us choice, Mister Morales . . .'—

Fifteen minutes later, see in a hidden room is Martin, who by now has beaten up Hugo's face. Up on Hugo's look be spotted some traces of blood, and he looks scared, slowly is disappointed in Martin. Despite Hugo began talking calmly' but is worried: 'You know something, McDermott, you disappoint me?'— Martin instead talks, his tongue is in cheek: 'Why is that, teacher Morales?'—

In a split second Hugo bows head down, and his mood alters to gloomy: 'Yes, I am a teacher! I always have tried to bring the best in a human . . . !'—

Saw Martin raises a hand up; as if intend to hit his ex-teacher: 'Ha-ha! I didn't give a shit about your lessons then, nor will I do as now?'—Crucially what be unsaid, while both look ineptly at one another. But, Martin spell out: 'I am only interested to find your bastard, Step-son?'—

Next Martin throws punches; but Hugo shifts away, when tries to untie hands behind his back: 'I don't know where Robert is? Even if I do, I wouldn't tell you . . .'—But Hugo is unable to finish his sentence, when Martin hits him. Smack! Hugo moans from pain. Martin then throws another punch. Ouch! He looks as if be cold-bloodedly, despite once ago he was Hugo's pupil, but keeps staring at Martin, with a sneer: 'You won't get out off me a thing, easily, Martin? I am only ashamed that once ago you were my student? Because you're unfeeling, and utterly a mad man, McDermott!'—Now Martin is fuming that, thrown more punches over Hugo's upper-body: 'Morales, better tell me, or your phishing wife will face an equal fate? If you know what I mean?'—Hugo turns aside, has tried to move around in the chair, and attempts to untie himself; while he make sense: 'Martin, don't you dare touch Rosalyn! Because she has nothing to do with that dealing . . .'—

33

Later that night, in the secure room, sees Rosalyn is lying upon bedcovers of the bed. On opposite side of the room view Nora, who sits on bed, whilst both women are talking about in a low voice?

In a flash the heavy door is got unlocked, and it gets open, whereas on the doorstep emerging Martin that, is walking in alongside a stranger. Seen as those two in Rosalyn jumps up out of a bed, and so does Nora. Then the two women alongside are moving closer, and resulting to embrace each-other. On the spot Martin is approached Rosalyn, when he grabs by her collar and does a powerful throw. It's unforeseen: Rosalyn doesn't hold her balance; as a result she falls down on the stony ground. In that case Nora yells; runs, then bends down, so as to pick her up. She is furious, and began speaking: 'Why in hell did you do it, Martin? Follow-up: he is set in motion, seated himself down onto Eleanor's bed corner; he then raises his head up, and reacts with a smirk, be ironic: 'Its reminder 'for you, Mrs. Morales, what I intend to do even worse with all of you are! Until someone in your family tells me where Rob is?'—Ensuing for Rosalyn raised her voice by abhors: 'I never thought that you Martin, can be thus heartless? You and my Rob were classmates! I would not dream to be kept a prisoner, for what?'—She is begun crying, still prolong with talking: 'The person, who must be punished Martin it's you, for the fears that you have inflicted on my family, but to Robert . . . !'—But Martin stops her, is teed off: 'We will catch him one way or the other, if he is alive? And when your dearest son Robert shows up, I would make sure send him to jail and Justice will be served!'—Resultant Rosalyn began weeping. Martin, impulsive signs to a man to Rosalyn, next at the door. Spur-of-the-moment Martin spoke, in a commanding voice: 'Ciao, Rosalyn, get out of here, do you hear me?'—

On a whim Nora jumps of bed; holds a fist in front, look as if set to spar. When she yells; her voice is edgy: 'You don't have guts to catch Robert?'—

Next she kicks Martin in the crouch. Ouch! Still be furious, Nora yells out: 'Don't you dare come near me? You will be paying dearly for it, Cyclops . . . !'—

CHAPTER 8

For the time being at the circus Rob became skilled at sleight of hand depends on the use half-dozen principles: for effects, routines and tricks, some of which Rob being able to learn herewith . . .

Like so a few months pass. It's a superb afternoon discover where be far-off Canada. Saw the sun is in zenith.

Rob, Dan and Gale interim, would perform routine in the Show. For now they signed a contract to perform the whole season, in the Circus.

Time in-between, in the Circus stall seen Wally is talking to Wallace: 'Sir, Sang and I are honored to perform in the Show, and if you allow us to try the new act? . . .'—

Wallace meanwhile, gave a beam, and is shaken with his head: 'Okay, Wally, today you are debuting! For starters, it is your Lucky day! I truly want your trio performing on the Days Show!'—

The Circus has observed five major Shows; is which Robert's acting called "Magic Magpie". Given that he and the magpie would go to perform in a huge tent, where being watched by those huge crowds . . .

The Circus program is adamant for the performers to move about on the trains, which have aboard alongside a double act with a magpie that are traveling in company of the artists that, would be performing in the afternoon Show with amusement.

This double act plus a magpie have been offered matching slates in acts and of themes at the Circus, where this trio would be performing under a tent in the Show.

CHAPTER 9

All but a month or two have past. Robert that now is called Wally, flanking Dan plus a magpie is in performance; and they would travel anywhere with the Circus that are scheduled for their routines . . .

Then, one evening out of circus tent has arrived Wallace, and in pleasing tone he is informing the duo: 'Your double act have a priority in our program for the show that features magpie Gale!'—

On a happy occasion Rob, who is now under a false name, Wally, reacted: 'I don't know what to say, sir?'—Next Wallace intruded: 'You're talented, Wally! Now, to the business, I am offering you is separate tours with our Circus, what do you say to that?'—Robert looks at Dan, and both are browsing pull up.

Next Robert came back with respond: 'Mister Wallace, we don't know our plans yet? As Mincius has said "We live not as we wish to, but as we can!"'—

Reflecting upon it, Wallace puts a smile; shivers his head; and is rejoining: 'Let's hope, Wally you're two can stay with the Show long enough?'—

At some stage of the Show Robert learned to perform Magic. Magician use one of the tricks termed sleight of hand'. Rob has chosen this specific type of innovative techniques, or tricks, and being featuring magpie, who is performing in the Circus.

Effect, by which Robert was performing, where him, the Magician is shown off play card that combined into a mysterious routine. Like so tricks that Rob would perform upon the ceiling as an acrobat, whilst Gale being acting, soaring over that crowd.

CHAPTER 10

A few months pass, since Robert and Dan have joined the Circus. During the time they would travel all around Canada with this show and all over. Across places they will be performing in the Shows, while like this featuring magpie Gale . . .

One day saw Robert and Dan stood sideways, near the Circus tent, where they are having a chat . . . While Robert spins, seems is uneasy that, whispers: 'Dan, how its going with gems? Did you find dealers to sell it?'—Dan ducks he's head down, when gave warning sign towards a man that walks by, and Rob is reacting: 'I see. Yep. Dan, be careful?'—Ensuing he again turns around; be wary: 'I have also set to make a deal with them . . . And I cannot go with you, Dan, cause of my rehearsals?'—Dan stops him, be firm: 'We have to find time for it? It's not easy with your rehearsals for the show, and I realize that? But, how can we go to the dealers without be seen by anyone?'—Hot on the heel, Rob shudders: 'I don't know, Dan? But we will think of something . . . ?'—Both think for a bit, silently: 'Where are the clients came from? Dan, can you trust them? You know that we have invested so much to sell them?'—Dan bows he's head down, and half-whispering: 'Do you think I don't know that? And yet, you will see, when we get there? That stuff must be sold one at the time or we might end up be in troubles?'—Rob looks at him, and puts a smile:

'Good thinking Danny boy!'—Dan gave alike beam; and hits Rob over with his upper arm: 'Would be better if we go together? Gale must not follow you, or it will put us in danger?'—Rob nods his head; is wary: 'I agree. Okay! Let's talk after my act?'—Robert bows to look down at his wristwatch. At the same time as Rob raised his head up, and gave a wink, he then murmurs: 'Dan, take care that all is set to seal the deal?'—In favor of a lucky gamble Dan produced a smile, when nods with his head.

Next seen both are walking off, but separate ways . . .

One night during the Shows the duo is wearing rags; and would pretend being superstars, so that no one can recognize them or find out of their identity . . .

PART II

CHAPTER 11

Almost six month pass by. In this part of the world is evening, but it has felt a frosty climate.

Meanwhile, at the Airport came into sight two male, one of which is an elderly causation man. As for the other he is an old Chinese male, who worn long match up robe, with a gray beard that, being on foot. Over Chinese man's face saw wrinkles; when he clings too a cane, and is under your own steam.

Those two elderly males still hang about at the airport; when oddly peek an aim counter; and they are instantly begun slowly approaching it.

Once the two old men have filled in required form. Ensuing next, as they are obtained their air tickets.

By their next effort both is getting through facing that Quarantine team; whereas on the spot an old man, who appeared is Robert, dropped his head down. One of that Airport staff gazes careful at the man: 'Why did you take a crow on your trip?'— The two aged men are feeling uncomfortable.

Now Chinese man pulls up his head, but does not hear them; and bows over the crow's in cage; he then puts a hand atop of birdcage. An eccentric old man happen is Dan. He does speak English, but in a false accent: 'This crow is my companion! I could never go away without my bird accompanied me!'—

Another from that quarantine staffs, emerge with a meticulous look: 'If you, please sir, pass the bird-cage for a check up?'—Given that Chinese man be dressed on to the nines, arise is Dan, and handed over to the staff a birdcage with a crow being inside of it.

Two hours pass as those two remain at the Airport, whereas are waiting in Quarantine to go through . . .

Meanwhile, a member of that quarantine rep looks oddly at Chinese man; next began checking the bird-cage, where a crow being set in. Then first from that Airport staff spins, facing Chinese man; and tells by logic: 'Okay! The crow is fine. We allow you two to board the plane!'—

He then turns, facing the rep, as shaken with his head; and is overt.

Fifteen minutes later a staff member reappears, and is declared: 'Let's get a bird-cage with your crow in, on board the plane!'—

Soon after this duo steps on the airplane, which is destined for Kong Hong; and it's ready to take off . . .

When dusk has surfaced, and covered the sky; where saw on the plane atypical Caucasian male, who advanced toward sits; and is passing through compound of rows. This man is seated down near plane's glass-sill; where adjacent to aged Chinese man, who too has taken a sit in the back, and is wearing on a South-East Asian traditional robe.

Later, during the flight an aged man sits near the woman of Chinese appearance. She looks be of short-to-medium, and is in her early or mid thirties. The woman is slim, well dressed; and being observing an aged man, who sits nearby her. The woman's name happen is Joanna that has a discussion in a brogue:

'Excuse me, sir, do you speak English?'—

For a minute the old man is tongue-tied, he then spins his thick neck, see to the travel companion.

Oddly to shed light on this aged man that appears is Robert, hearing his voice in hoarseness: 'Yeah, of course I do!'—But he tries to break: Lady, where you're traveling to?'—The Chinese woman grins; and looks closely in his eyes, guessed if she's mistaken. Given her body leans toward him that, she prolongs with a chat: 'I am flying to Hong Kong, where I will go off, and by my next route travel to Macau. What's your plans, sir?'—Robert seems is ill at ease; and by taken breaths he tries to relax. He then turns aside, as if being unsure, but a lilt is betrayed him: 'Well, I do not know yet!'—

Rob seems is edgy; when spins and angles, and points at this old Chinese man wore robe, for backing: 'Do you see this old man behind us?'—

On a whim Joanna spins around to view the man: Yes! Are you two acquainted, by a chance?'—Rob moved his head be unsettled: 'Spot-on, we are acquainted. In fact, I am escorting him to Hong Kong!'—

While this Chinese man here produces a smile, like so ducks with his fake beard three times.

CHAPTER 12

Be on board the plane for many hours, this duo and a
magpie have landed at daytime: now they reach their
destination that is Hong Kong.

Given that in the Hong Kong Airport, seen as those travelers
have disembarked, along with this duo.

By this duo's next move, they are walking toward carousel, so
as to pick up their baggage from.

With two hours pass, still remained at the Airport be in
the quarantine, Rob now called Wally is walking beside Ming
that dressed in weird; it's a good thing he has got a fake beard
upon his face. Now Rob sees a chance; and a start murmur to
Dan, but covers his mouth: 'Will it sink for the apt staff that
we have hidden things in the secret compartment on the base of

bird-cage?'—Dan be a fake old man, bows his head down; and is begun coughing, in between covering his lips. Then he whispers to Robert: 'Pray, they do not find it!'—

This duo is proceeding next to register at that aimed check-in counter, at the Airport.

Soon after this duo is having got a brief delay in the Quarantine. Just then, one of that apt staff looks thoroughly at Dan, who is holding a cane, and began talking in a brogue English: 'I see, but you don't need a visa, sir.'—Next the official, who appears is mistrusting Robert switches see to him. In its place he raise his up eyebrows; and signs toward Rob be called Wally: 'Having said all, you have not got a valid visa to stay in Hong Kong?'—On the spot, this duo is standing with tongue-tied, since their grown being on alert.

With over fifteen minutes pass, one amid that staff peek Dan, who is holding a cage with a crow inside?

Resultant the staffs are having observed Dan and Rob's suitcases.

Decisively an official states just to Robert: 'Sorry for the delay, sir! Your luggage seem be with our standard!'—

With another twenty-minute passes, eventually the Official is stated to them: 'It is approved overall for your bird-cage! Enjoy your stay in Hong Kong!'—

Up to Midday this duo still remains in Airport.

There saw: Sign > Rob and Dan are having left restroom, located inside the Airport's complex.

Up-to-the-minute those two are having changed appearances, with the purpose that nobody would be able to identify of their schemes?

Unless without check-out the double act is unaware that, Joanna too has not left the airport, yet . . .

A sudden she approaches the duo, is assumed by gestures toward Dan; given that her being ready to reveal of their identity . . . Unless Joanna began talking in Cantonese to Dan: 'Who are you? What your two 'intend by arriving in Hong Kong?'—Dan bows head down; but his face turned pink; when hearing he's well-spoken English: 'My friend and I came to Hong Kong on business! And, we will appreciate if you don't tell anyone, what you saw then and now on two of us changed looks?'—Here, Dan gave a hint to Robert, and slants aside to look at the side. Awkwardly both parties are standing froze among anguished, how to react. Joanna puts wide smile, with a stare at Robert, like cat on butter. In that case she raises, like is inquisitive; seen her upper-body is shaken: 'Is your name Wally for real? Or it's not?'—Robert is self-conscious, and ducks his head; then his face turned pink. She beams; takes breathes; then Rob is breaking awkwardness, and talks being wary: 'Why do you want to know?'—But Joanna stops him; then be tied in with them; as it seems is inquisitive: 'We two are foreigners.'—She then shakes with her upper-body; when looks into his eyes; Joanna beams: 'I was in your state, 'now you're in China?'—Be puzzled, Robert inclines his head, it appears is agreed. As he talks slowly, but is calm: 'You spot-on! My name is Wally Miser! What is your name?'—This woman leans her head toward him; gave a big smile; when she retorts: 'Well, I like your new appearance better now, then earlier, Wally!'—She gave a beam so as to allure him: 'My name is Joanna Hoi Pereira!'—She then is discontinued of talking. Robert seems is at a complete loss forthwith, as a result of her staring, avowed: 'I don't follow you, Joanna?'—Joanna instead talks loud, so as to sham him: 'Don't you dare discriminate me?'—Rob at that moment has felt embarrassed; but tries to break up a dead lock; when his upper arms be shaken; it's made sense to retort, with him being timid: 'I don't discriminate you! It is just doesn't sink for me?'—Joanna looks in his eyes; is breathing deep, when tells gently: 'My family originated in era, when the Portuguese had invaded Macau . . .'—In quirk of fate, she acquaints them with a tale of her family's legacy . . . She then adds-on to her tale: 'I am half Macau Portuguese and half Chinese! Can you tell apart, in a flash or not?'—Except Robert, who seeming is stunned, yet attentive; for him breathing deeply; for he saying in a shaky voice: 'You strike for me a chord of stunning me!'—With respect she grins, and her impression is exciting: 'What if I tell you that, I speak both Portuguese and Cantonese! Will that blow up your mind more?'—At this point, Robert seems is confused, and given the impression of being at a complete loss. He takes in air; then snaps: 'I don't know, what you have meant, Joanna?'—Be out of her depth she produced a grin; stares at him, does with explaining, as murmurs close into his ear: 'I meant if you will be interested to come visit me in my place of work? When you pass through Macau, Wally? Do you swear come to see me in Macau's Casino?'—Rob picks up his left hand; and folds it up to his upper body; he swears, but is amused: 'I do! Cross my heart . . .'—

Chapter 13

It's a divine warm day in Hong-Kong. Robert and Dan before now, checked in a hotel, be located Downtown on inner skyscraper that, has got luxury.

After having relaxed in their hotel-suit; and taken a shower, this duo made request from hotel's admin for a map around Hong Kong.

Before long they went on an excursion.

Here came into sight Robert and Dan are walking through the center. There across they meet the sun that is flashing with its rays from the skies, and the climate is a tropical for tourist to enjoy it.

After twenty-five minutes on walk, they came within reach of this shop, where it is observed an advert 'Mr. Wong-Lao Wu Jewelry Store'. The jewelry store is located in a narrow lane.

Vision this duo moved toward aimed Jewelry store, Robert in a flash looks around, and bends his head down to double-check it; he then is tackling Ming: 'Dan, are you sure this is the right address, we have got here?'—In that case Dan takes over a note pad, his head down; as double-checks, when he slants down so as to look at note: 'Yep! This is the place, all right. Wally who is Chinese you are or I am?'—Rob ducks his head; then slaps over Dan's arm of jacket. As he gave a grin, and says be certain: 'Naturally you're partner, no doubt about it?'—

Prior to barge in, once more they are browsed warily. Next without delay they are walking into the store, where signal of a din activates, as it's being created particularly of musical timbre, with sound coming back.

Dins reach the Chinese owner who's emerged over from behind the counter. This man is materialized a senior, and medium tall, and worn on informal. In the store jewels are affixed, while put on display inside glass-sills for a safety net.

There come into sight a stockpile that by an assortment of range be filled with gems. Given that owner is behind the counter, saw Rob walks beside Dan, whilst they are coming within an inch of Wong Lao.

Dan began at once talking in Cantonese: 'Good day! Do you speak English, sir?'—The Chinese man raises his up head, and looks at this duo in silence.

Something made sense to him, and Wong gave a grin; ducks his head; then spoke nicely: 'Yes! 'How can I help you?'—Rob slants his head; signs to Dan and looks as if it has meant that, he want to make the deal alone. Given Wong's hand lies on his upper-body: 'I am Mister Wong Lao, owner of this store!'—Hot on the heel Rob looks at Dan, as they both are became embarrassed, in silence. Next Robert speaks slowly; but is daring: 'Mister Wong, as you know fate plays role in our life that, has brought us here. For we were sent to you by a mutual supplier?—At this time Wong corners, as looks at the two; then flattens his upper arm, but seems is puzzled: 'What is it that you want?'—Those two are ducked their heads of consent.

Rob puts a hand in his pocket, and removes wrapped bag; is unwrapped it. Then he lays that heap down on the glass counter . . .

On the spot without warning sound starts buzzing. Sees some customers entered this store. On the spot this trio is at brink of panicky. In that case Wong quickly removes Rob's heap away, and hides it under his counter . . .

. . . Once the customers have left, Wong re-appeared up from under the counter. He looks be composed, with a wide smile, seen as he puts reading glasses up on. Resulting Wong takes out from lower than windowsill of the shelf's a magnifying glass that he wisely handles, so as to observe it. Afterward Wong deals with the two: 'Let me have a look at that stuff, then we will talk about?'— The duo looks at each-other, duck with their heads, and they are waiting keenly for an expert of high-quality jewels . . .

A while passes since Wong scans that possession one at the time? Next the Chinese dealer raises his head up; puts a smile, is concentrating on the duo; it's being after all a long wait. Wong looks up, and is eager: 'So, gentlemen, how much do you want to sell that stuff for?'—

Robert deals with Wong alone: 'Mister Wong, how much do you think pure gold together with jewelry worth it?'—Given that Wong's appearance has shown he's being on safeguard.

A period of time passes, since both parties are trying to make a deal . . .

Soon after both parties seal the deal. A sudden Robert made a query, in sweet talks: 'My apology, sir, but my friend here and I are not familiar with the locale area! And so, we need a job! Do you know if someone can provide a safe job for both of us?'—Wong looks as if infers rather odd; he then turns see to Dan with a grin; and says be witty: 'Why you both have not trying to find jobs in Macau?'—

In next to no time Robert followed by Dan's shaken hand with Wong, when the duo is walking off, before open the door: 'It's nice meeting you, Mister Wong! And be profitable too, for both of us!'—

Still it's sunny daytime: after the two have got news of their transfer from Hong-Kong to Macau on a Chinese ferryboat . . .

Happily, by the next travel Robert in the company of Dan is roving on a vessel, which is a Chinese made ferryboat, in sunlight hours.

The crossing to Macau on the ferryboat takes them approximately forty-five minutes.

CHAPTER 14

I t's a picturesque, warm evening in Macau. The lavender color-covered sky is filled with stars. The climate is of a low humidity.

Here came into sight Macau's Casino, where oblique have existed apart a Bar that, any can visit.

Meanwhile, interior of the Bar behind counter, seen Joanna is running the joint, by filling glasses for those clienteles, who are kept coming in hostelry, it's like kind of a drinking hole. Given regulars are sitting at the tables: that it's a full house in there.

Inner of a bar hear lively piece of music be played to that, business is booming.

Surprisingly Rob and Dan entered the Bar, where two be seated down near the counter. Opposite from them over the counter Joanna is in motion back and forth and providing the regulars with alcohol or some soft drinks.

Joanna meanwhile, keeps in mind that are involved those two, for Robert that is Wally, above all.

For the time being, Robert is clumsy, when shyly has ordered drinks from Joanna, who stood behind counter: 'Can I get two specs of lemonade, please?'

Joanna looks at him, be puzzled: 'Wally, don't you want to drink slightly stronger than like Vodka?'—

On the spot Robert shy's away: 'Oh, no thanks! I am not a drinker!'—Thence she spins, and curves upfront to pour Robert and Dan drinks. Given Joanna stands with back to him that pulls out a packed in plastic out from her sleeve; then she's spiked Robert, so-called Wally his drink.

Given Robert naïve that, is unaware of Joanna Hoi conduct?'—

Still in the bar, Joanna shifts glasses full with drinks one by one to Dan, and second for Robert. She puts a smile, hears, her being charismatic. Saw next that Joanna pulls out cigarettes from a pack; and offers those two to smoke; it follows that she lights up a single for herself. Robert is shaken head like shy's away; for the reason that he thinks it's useless. When next he is yelling: 'Oh, no thanks, I don't smoke!'—Joanna is bewitching: 'Wally, don't be a child! Be a real man! What make sense that a few shots of liquor won't spoil you! Trust me!'—

Next she is taken his hand in hers; it looks as if charmingly into Robert's eyes . . .

Soon the whole thing turn of vague impression; and Robert is feeling as if all rounds faded away; his eyes weakened; he then began to forget about all . . .

Chapter 15

Robert is in Daydream: it's like a time traveled him into the past. See at this point Robert is in return to the USA. After he has left the railway wagon; and is now on his way toward Eleanor's country house . . .

A strong sunray has blinded him up out from a glow; thus he covers his eyes over with one hand . . .

. . . Robert before now is walking quite a few miles across alleyway. He then does a stop, looks around; while exhales in the dew. The places are flowering. Up on the Low Valley and around, observed layers, whereas still are covering with fluffy snow . . .

Now hear Robert's voice: "I have come in this old cottage. Nora is meeting me on doorstep. I will be taken Nora's hand in my, and held her in my arms. I want to tell her my version of dealing! Then I would give Nora lots of money . . . Later I will pack her stuff up, and we both are fleeing! Cause it kills me being part from her! I long for her!

Eleanor! Where are you?'—

Here Robert reminisces, of what come to his mind . . .

Soon his hallucinations ended. Robert's dreams have got disrupted?

Now and there is Joanna's place; it'd early morning hour. Here came into the view Robert that lies next to Joanna, in her bedroom; without he is figured out of being tricked: he does not remember from the time when, how he has got in the house, most important into Joanna's bed? Which has caused him such effect deceptive from night before, when he was intoxicated, or not?

Abruptly flash back Robert's memory: it brings to mind what has ensued yesterday with him?

Here in reality saw the moon vanishes. Still a glow from glass fall on Grandfather's Clock that be heard with bangs, and it's showing time: 4.30 a.m.

Sudden a person's cell phone began buzzing! That noise has made Wally jumping up off the bed. But next he learns that call has not meant for him?'—

Hear Joanna talks over the phone, in Cantonese: 'Hello!'— She stops; still listens to one on other side of the phone line. Next Joanna starts talking again: 'Yes. It's she speaking! Who's it?'—A man's voice on the phone tells her about aim of his call?

Joanna talks again on the phone: 'Who? Aha, is it you, Hau?'—She stops short; and listens to a man's voice on the line, then in a tense voice came her respond: 'Yes, I did call you for a job in . . .'—Though now she is listening warily to a man's voice; then covers phone with her palm; spins facing Wally, and tackles Robert of doubt softly, but ardently: 'Can you play any instrument?'—Robert moves his head up and down: 'Yes, I do! I play the guitar!'—In this case she puts a smile, and prolongs: 'How about before a live audience by singing? Will you shy away?'—Wally shakes with his head: 'No, I used to perform in a Circus!'—Rob is with a nervy smile; bob his head; looks if all were arranged for him. She motions back; and is prolonging of chatting on the phone: 'So, does he need to get ready for the job, right now?'—She listens; then angles to a handbag in silence; and takes out a pen, along with a notebook from inside. Next Joanna responses: 'Yeah. Ah-ha, I know! Just a second! Let me get a pen to write it 'down . . .'—Joanna leans over, and reaches for the pen and a notebook. She then wrote something in it.

A minute ago Joanna ended a phone discussion; she then gets up of the bed, is in motion to bathroom.

After she returns on the spot seed her body skin is soaked. On top she is wore on top a robe.

Once Joanna's eyes see Robert, and she is frozen in a flash; her breath be caught in. Subsequently she takes gulps of air, to calm hers desires down.

She instantly rolls bunch of hair by way of her head aside; and is seeking Rob-Wally to initiate? No doubt Joanna likes him a lot, and she's felt bliss being filled of butterflies, in her stomach . . .

Robert meanwhile, is walking round and seeking things, which he has lost on the evening before; because it sinks to him what ensued then and there . . .

The instant Robert picks up his rags that be laid everywhere. Joanna in contrast is eager to have him again, and breaks ineptness amid them, when gently: 'Wally, what are looking for?'—Though Robert evaluates in his mind; but doesn't pay attention to her, while is kept seeking . . .

Joanna is moody: 'Where are you going, Wally?'—

Without lifting his head, Robert became timid and tense; as he's responding: 'You told me that I was 'invited for a job interview, so am I ready to go now. There would-be a vacancy for my friend that he can excessively find for himself?'—Except for she can't deem, what he has said so as to break the ice. Hot on the heel, she is enhanced by full of meaning. Joanna is feeling passionate, when she talks loud: 'Wally, do you want to leave now?'—As Rob is firm: 'Yes! Now, it's practically daylight! Since I am not familiar with Macau's sites? It's most likely, when I get there, it is going to be Midday?'—

When Robert walks to the exit, and does make a stop; he then turns; bows his head down, like he is shamed: 'Thank you for a lot, Joanna! And, ciao!'—Joanna in contrast sees Wally is parting, but it doesn't make sense to her; yet she yells toward his back: 'Who is Nora?'—Spur-of-the-moment she raises her head, it seems to be nosy; but jealous too. Then it has struck her: 'Don't rush, Wally! Take the keys from my car? Here it is . . .'—As on her voice via echo, or after this is hanged in the air.

Next Joanna's mood has changed; and she gladly is plunged into the bedding . . .

CHAPTER 16

Robert being called Wally begun working in Macau's Casino recently; and by now has received a uniform intent for suchlike premises . . .

Given that Robert just arrived in the Casino, and is walking right on the night shift. Next without delay, he is progressed into the Gaming-room . . .

Later that night, in the Gaming room sees a vast crowd of merrymaking. View those men are wearing dinner suits, seen as the women being dressed in a modern fashion. There's flash of illuminations that be installed up on the stage exclusively for the celebrities'.

Not far see Dan, who is into betting at Roulette Table . . .

Once Wally has peeked Dan there, he is on foot, when coming up to him. Next he began whispering something vital to Dan; given that Rob bends down, closer toward this last one. Wally bows his body down a tad: 'Put your bet on eighteen; next gamble with eleven red; after is putting chips on eight, white, and on black.'—

Suddenly it sinks to Dan, he bobs his head; puts half-a-smile; and acts as if Rob is unfamiliar to him.

On a whim Dan gets up of his sit, and sendoff without stop.

Period in-between, Robert doesn't suspect that, a strange man is probing him, where he stood; but is getting ready to walk off toward sideways . . .

Just over time passes, it's far past mid-night . . .

Up-to-the-minute Dan has won a large amount on a Roulette table; advantageously he is receiving lay claim with a great deal of hard cash . . .

In next to no time Robert gets around, where Dan is placed, and he attempts to support this last one winning. Dan bows down so as to whisper: 'That win was an easy one. Spot-on'!'—A Robert named Wally acts as if has not focused on Dan; in its place he stood to the side. On a whim he nods his head; is mumbling: 'Who's said it would be difficult?'—

Robert in its place, curves his body down; looks at Dan, and winks.

Time in between Dan moves toward anew game, where he is trying to win on Poker-machines.

One hour later has gone by. Snappily Joanna's drawn near Wally; it seems is resulted to talk, she says charmingly: 'Wally, after that night we become as one, but I don't see you anymore?'— Instead he's irate: 'Don't expect you ever will, Joanna! It was slipup that you're and I? Not . . .'—Joanna cuts him short; is charming: 'Why? I thought we have got closer'—Rob is ironical; but firm: 'If Confucius would say: "Men screw with dicks, women screw with minds!"—Rob shuts up on the spot; then says at last: 'So, I believe this is goodbye, dear! Have to 'go. I am busy working, you know that?'—

. . . See there is a winner in the Casino. All rounds gambling, the others are drinking Champagne; from the stage heard, where music to be played. This is Rob that, performing up on the stage for audiences . . .

At the same night, once Wally has ended on Casino's stage, saw one among those guests encircled him.

Hear those guests are discussing the winner here, who happens, is Dan; whilst has involved: 'I was thinking tonight this winner is a lucky bastard, don't you agree?'—

The entrepreneurs, made signs with their eyes are shown at Dan, who accompanies a man. A guest in his turn shaken up his upper arm; is leering, and re-joins in an English accent: 'I really didn't think about it?'—This first guest is out of his depth, when gave a wink; but being witty: 'Go, and tell to my niece a fairy-tale? Just as we speak, she is getting ready for bed! She could believe you!'—

At the same very moment a few good looking young women come up to the gents footing are encircling that grouping. This second guest leers, looks like he is fancying her: 'Gentlemen, look who we are having here?'—Those men spin as one, to look at womanly. Saw the womanly are dressed in silky garment, via which it being spotted their bare figures. Given that bunch of men is attentive to those prostitutes.

Hear next one of the womanly' is begun chatting, in the company of those men. One of the women pokes fun; but speaks English with an accent: 'Good evening, good-looking man! Would you like to have a good time?'—Those men are produced beaming, as one of the guests that she has tackled, puts a smile; he is in sweet-talking goes making for his move: 'Hello, there! I would love to! Let's have a drink? What do you like, my dear?'—Follow-up a first guest joins in teasing implying to one of womanly . . .

Out of the blue Joanna becomes visible to those parties, be seen Robert in the company of them. In common with other a second guest turns facing Wally, and gave the lowdown: 'Wally would you entertain yourself, if you are the winner, wouldn't you?'—On a whim Robert leans his head; and responds being shies away, yet he is cynical: 'Well, gentlemen you are amazed me! You won't make to be noticed? Ha-ha! What in the civil society is going to say about your fight?'—Yet, Joanna cuts him short; while with a nervy smile, she has tagged him by arm sleeve; snaps as if her being hurt: 'Wally, you have said more than enough! If you don't believe them, it's your problem?'—Next she ineptly grabs Rob's arm, and on a critical point, and began dragging him away to sideways.

He is panting; though waits for Joanna to tell him more. Joanna is contrary earnest: 'I am protecting you, Wally? If it wasn't for me, you would never be hired, in this Casino?'—She then signs by her eyes toward this second man from company. Now Joanna has a word to add: 'By the way, you see the man standing to the right, he is the Boss here!'—On the spot Robert turns to face this man amid that group. See that Robert is produced a nervy smile from a shock; and gave the unknown man the lowdown, but in sweet talks: 'My apology for the former remarks, sir? It's meant to be a joke?'—Wally bows his head down; and is prolonged in sweet-talking: 'Sir, am I working on night shift tomorrow, or which one?'—

From nowhere a typical looking Englishmen is coming within reach of that company with Robert, and get direct involved in the conversation. This is Ron Swift that looked at these parties; he then flattens his upper arm. Seen Ron comes near Rob's standing, and is emitting: 'Good evening!'—

Swift signs to Dan, be curio and sly: 'Wasn't this young man be lucky?'—It follows that Robert bobs with his head; Swift then prolongs of talking: 'And with your help, young man?'—Robert seem is confused: 'Sir, I don't understand, what you have said? I am not acquainted with . . .'—But Swift stops him; spins by facing Robert, and is asked him over: 'Okay. Do you work here?'—Like so Robert puts a smile; when moves his heads up and down: 'Yes I am, sir! Can I help you?'—Swift shakes his neck: 'Maybe! Do you are two having come from US?'—Robert affirms with a nod: 'Yes, I did I speak only for myself. How did you know?'—In that case Swift angles his head toward Dan, and is extend a big finger up. This Englishman gave a wink; by shaken his head; he then is rejoining: 'A lucky guess. Talking about your friend, it would be a shame since the man has won, as if you two have gone, and forgotten?'—Up-to-the-minute is silent. Next Ron tells Robert:

'Listen, my young friend, Joanna knows a great deal about gambling!'—It hits Robert at once; he opts to whisper, but have of fret: 'I don't know what is you meaning, sir?'—Seen Swift sneers, as it gave the impression that he's endorsed it, a look is sure: 'What I meant is, I will tell you two, when 'we are meeting next time?'—

Here Ron turns around, and began talking to other gentlemen: 'What you're valued the most, when you are made a bet, gentlemen?'—

All at once the Casino's manager advances to Rob; then he butts in, makes hand-gestures: 'Wally, you not are going to perform?'—Now Wally is relieved:

'Yes, sir! I will go now, and get ready for! . . .'—

On a critical point Robert decide to escape Swift; but this last one has stopped him, alone says arrogantly: 'I want to make you an offer working for me?'—Robert at once is feeling out of the ordinary; when his cheeks changed to pink: 'Thank you, sir but I have a job, right here, in this Casino!'—Swift pays attention to this duo, for a moment or two sound was activated; he then says decisively: 'You know, something young man, you and I will meet again!'—Robert emerges be tense by a dare, thus he snapped: 'How do you know that we will meet again?'—Swift resultant, has responded, hearing his voice is firm: 'Oh, I am sure we will, young man! Authentically a good deal could be read 'about you're up on your temple?'—Robert senses on the spot that something is not right. Swift disrupts his thoughts; and raises his voice, is sweet-talking: 'I did not catch your name, yet?'—In a difficult situation Wally is stuttering: 'Ro . . . Aha, my name is Wally Miser?'—Given that Swift browse is pulled up: 'Wally, is this your name, chap?'—Robert instead moves his neck up and down; still he is disturbed. Spotting next, Swift is turning your back on their discussion.

CHAPTER 17

Since a meeting chanced, like this a few days pass.

Currently is Robert's day off that, he's used for outing through Macau. See Rob sits beside Dan on a trishaw (tricycle) that, has driven from side to side of Macau . . .

From nowhere on the road appears a "Mercedes". This auto stops near this double act is standing.

Sighted the car-door opens outward, whilst from gets off Swift, who has smoked a cigar.

Given that Robert has met this man during his night shift . . . Saw the same time as Swift came within reach of Robert be called Wally, without his forward. Ron looks be cocky: 'So, I have said that the two of us, are going to meet? Didn't I?'—On the spot Robert gave the impression of being disturbed. Hear Swift is snoopy: 'What you said your name was? The last time we

78

have met, I forgot what it is?'—Robert talks slowly and carefully: 'Wally Miser, sir . . .'—But Swift stares at Rob; is thinking a tad; when puts a grin be smug; and he asking with biting wits: 'Wally, is it your real name? You see, I have connections, as well be on familiar terms with police and Interpol that, were seeking Rob Lipinski?'—Robert's face changed to pale; as he is staring at Ron Swift. Swift prolong, is teasing: 'Before I forget, by the way, are you happened to be the same man, the Cops in the hunt for?'—

Now Robert's tongue-tied feels as if his be trapped that, stared is wishy-washy. Now Swift sees a chance to nail him, when says with biting wits: 'Why we not give there a call, and find out? Where there will have a chat with you, they know how? You don't mind, Wally, if I call them now? Why you were turned pale, lad?'—A talk Robert is gauche, and tense: 'Yep! You have got spot-on! It's me! So what?'—Robert then turns around is edgy, and prolonged: 'Mister Swift, what do you want? I don't know, maybe you want to make a scandal here?'—In that case Swift began laughing: 'You wrong! Absolute not, I have no intention my young friend!

'Au contraire, I have big plans for you . . .'—Thus Rob has declared, be still ill at ease: 'Really? And, what it is to you, who

I am?'—On a whim Swift with biting wits, as talks loud: 'If you want me to forget all about your existence, Wally? Do you hear, lad, you owe me a small favor?'—Now Rob is at complete lost; he stares, and act in respond. On the spot he stutters: 'What sort of favor?'—

Swift sucks in air; and looks as if he is superior over him; he then talks in jingle: 'Let's just say, you need to bring me box of jewelry, few million in cash, and gold bullion from the Casino's safe, where you're working now! That is not so hard to do it, Wally?'—Be probed. Wally looks at Swift; and became demoralized: 'Who in hell told you that, I am a burglar?'—They are looking on each-other, as if being ready to clash. Swift is ironic, but being edgy, and talks quietly: 'What are you humming? By the way, do you know someone with the nickname Cyclopes, from Interpol?'—On the spot Robert turn panicky; when he snuffled; and nod his head:

'I have worked my butt off for . . .'—But Swift stops him; while his tongue-in-cheek: 'Being expert in this kind of thing, it wouldn't be hard to do the job?'—In a flash Swift lights a cigar, is smoking and blowing out; he then made rings of smoke that flew in the air. Both parties are tongue-tied for a moment or two;

and is resulted: 'So, what is going to be, Wally? Say yes, you agree to do the job?'

Later at sunset, Robert stood on the bridge next to Dan, and they are chewing the fat, as both looking down from a bridge into the water. Reflection of its flashing lights is well-lit beneath, whereas sponging across metropolis. As Robert is saying softly, of fret: 'You see Dan, we have stuck in deep shit? What am I going to do, now?'—Robert and Dan are thinking for a jiffy. Dan is appearing uneasy: 'Then again if you refuse to go ahead with Swift's plan, Interpol and the police could catch, you! And, they will put me in jail next to your sell! You don't have a choice as to accept it!'—

CHAPTER 18

The weather in Macau follows the calendar, and it's hour of darkness. The sky is full of shooting stars, while it is felt warm due to a tropical climate.

Rob has arrived in an automobile at the Macau's Casino, where see Dan is seated inside too. Given they were having rented the car, earlier that day. When this double act steps out of the car; still both have remained for a tad outside for a chat. Dan turns to look around; when he whispers, be edgy: 'Wally, you just only arrived on the night shift? No matter how, but Swift will know! Given that we both are under surveillance . . .'—

A sudden Swift's watchdog that worked for him came within reach of this duo; and he budges into their chitchat. Though this watchdog is snooping: 'Who are you talking about?'—Be caught unawares Dan looks at Robert; when this last one gave a smirk; and alone alleged, be ironic: 'Gee, let me think? I was talking about the same thing, Mister Swift!'—This watchdog proceeds; first looks around, then murmurs to this duo like assumed as is chewing the fat: 'Believe me, you have been watched! Consistent with you, Mister Swift is enemy for all that lives and breath? For your information he has planned the whole thing all-alone! In case if something goes wrong?'—Robert is self-assured; and badges in: 'Maybe it is not far all, what your Mister Swift wants us to get into!'—

Later on Robert enters the gaming room, where view those visitors are addicted to betting in.

Robert instead, has left; apparent is going to the security station; just as those guests in their cars crossed into the Casino's site . . .

Something like ten minutes pass Robert walks into the Security station; where without delay hears him being talking to another strange man.

Robert then alone in sweet talks: 'Lie, I forgot my ID card at home! Can you lend me yours, please? Unless the cameras apt at me, to catch-22?'—

Given a second watchdog looms in that stations X-rays him thoroughly. Seen man be cool, with a smirk, and he's alleged: 'Wally, don't forget my 'night shift is finishing roughly in an hour?'—Rob bows his body down, looks at his wristwatch, and nods his head. Rob is under pressure, as tried to walk off: 'This wouldn't take long! Don't worry about a thing!'—Lie takes breaths; looks at Rob; and spanks him. He takes out a magnet key (card) of his jacket pocket, and gave it over to him. Given Lie is the second watchdog that seems is on edge: 'I hope so! Good luck, man! Go faster: one foot here and another . . .'—

There came into sight the main access of Macau's Casino, this built has a triple store or higher. Other builds and security rooms that were well hidden from strangers among surround site.

Meanwhile, at the main entry seen a few admin bodies. Robert's felt clumsy; but his breath is caught in on that occasion; following he breathes out. Like so one amid bosses tries to picture as if Robert is. Given that first Controller is ironic, with a wink: 'So, did you sort out with this 'Macanese woman? Does she have more sex with you?'—Wally placed a smirk, like so be ironic: 'Listen, as Confucius has said "I hear and I forget. I see and I remember. I do and I understand!" She doesn't have windows! It's not for me! No way!'—

Next he gave him a wink; shakes with his upper arms. Seen after, Rob under false name Wally is turned your back on something.

Ten minutes later, Rob has approached facade of the Casino's entrance, where without hesitation he is sweeping up his ID of that key-card . . .

Wally moans; is tense, and speaks up: 'If in the decision-making understood that ID is not mine? I will be in deep shit!'—Dan appears be nervous: 'You see, this is to be no-winning situation?'—

A sudden crow has flown in; where it is made chaos . . .

Spur-of-the-moment it is silent. Then Rob saw a chance for him and Dan to proceed with dealing; he murmurs, as is tense: Let's hurry up, Dan! Go-go!'—

Robert next gestures to Dan, view leans head toward the exit.

Dan on a whim whispers, be curious: 'Wally, how we are going to open a magnetic bolt?'—

Hot on the heel, those two are thinking; while both being breathless.

It looks as if Wally is assured, when he talks: 'I have thought of it, and got an idea! Let's stick to the plan? Those security guys are having swiping cards? And, so we need to . . .'—

Robert immediately calls for Gale, as resonate of his yell be heard around. Ensuing he turns facing a magpie and Dan: 'Follow me, Gale! You too, Dan!'—

View Dan, who gave the impression of being dazed: 'What if anyone sees us both?'—

. . . In next to no time a duo is under your own steam, with no talking, and non-stop. Wally looks be grim, but focused: 'Can you lever me a glow, Dan?'—Dan is edgy: 'Okay. But I won't you be put at risk!'—

Now Robert gave a nervy laugh; and says be cocky: 'What are you scared of? Wait for me behind the close doors, if you're neurotic! Since both of us 'could be detected by these cameras?'—

On the spot Wally swipes a key card through this magnetic system that is suitable, and has to be regenerated by a flip of getting to open it . . .

Soon Rob walks alone in the surveillance Centre. Here is the Control room, where seed screens are filled with loads of monitors, which have been connected to these cameras. The Centre reminds of a spacecraft; all over the place is operating if to be set in motion by having a great deal of push buttons, through elucidation control are aimed switching on and off overall . . .

Though Lights off there, but Rob easily is watching around, by making use of a torch.

Wally seems be thrilled: 'Whoa! That's amazing! I am not surprised no one has access in there? How much of goods are in there? Nora and my sister 'will be ecstatic, here!'—

. . . Robert sneaks through the Control room, and has worn on black gloves. Seen his head are covered with a mask; given that velvet box is hidden within excess of these windshields . . .

By taken a deep breath, Robert sits down to look at the monitor.

A minute passes since Rob broke-in that considered by him it's a long time. Like so he began searching for a correct password. He browses, and is spotting a safe by way of attempting to crack that code too. He bears by working hard, but without a clue how to break into database? Except the heavy door doesn't open it; for Rob is trying a combination lock.

In a critical point Robert shudders, even if he is tied, but tried breaking in: 'It doesn't make sense?'—

Intuitively he thinks of anew method . . .

Observing Robert's face it has expressed amazement, like so he mumbles, be keen: 'I never have got lucky with so many treasures? Whoa! I wish to 'break into that safe?'—

Sudden it hits him: 'Okeydokey! I will try anew code, then?'—Like so Wally murmurs to himself: 'It is all-odd in there? I have to be careful . . .'—

Then without losing a second Robert is determined to proceeding with anew programs at the PC . . .

To Robert's luck the access is letting slowly get open. On a happy occasion, he is elated, and mumbles to himself: 'Eureka!'—

Given that Rob cracks the codes, he is succeeding a windshield opens.

Next he's enhancing, where is able to remove a box be packed with costume jewelry . . .

By Robert next go is succeeding, and he gaining an access to cash from the giant safe, which currency observed in $ Patacas (Macau State-run currency).

With easy-going Robert 1s found bullion with gold, estimated of over $US 2 Million in cash, and time be close to 11.30 PM.

Ensuing without more ado he opens a dark sack, in which he places bullion of gold, along with cash. He is observing bag upper tear, which covers with a jewelry box, with distribution of shared cash. Be hereafter pleased with that job Robert has closed the loaded sack with a zipper; he then escapes . . .

Be out of walls Rob under your own steam, listened, but is guarded. He is in motion toward exit, except him being unseen by anyone beside for cameras.

He alongside Dan in back listens alertly for those approaching footsteps of it's noises.

Around fifteen minutes pass, seen Wally like a Ghost gets into the Casino's parking lot, where as well cameras to be installed. Despite trying, he has detached earlier; still only a minute left for him to flee without be caught on the spot . . .

Spur-of-the-moment he puts a rich sack into the car booth that, knew it would be ready available to go; alike silently, Robert then locks car stall behind.

Robert returns from the car-park, he goes straight to work; and now is in performance for a stunt, when begun singing on Casino's stage . . .

Chapter 19

Later that night Robert sits in the interior of a car, and is driving on full speed, like a madman.

Seen Dan is seated at the front sit beside Rob, this last one has felt nervy; thus he yells: 'What are you doing? Don't press hard on breaks, Wally? This is not your car you know, we have rented it?'—

Given that Wally still looks ahead on the road, and handholds steering wheel, while he is responding: 'Who gives a toss? Bloody Ron! I have never been a crook. Thank God, no one saw any or me did it? You were outside the door, Dan? Did you see anyone passing through you?'—Dan takes a deep breath; and looks at Robert, then raises his head up; when he reacts: 'No I haven't! Thank God! Someone has said pray to God for your lost soul, buddy!'—

As Robert has coordinated held on speeding wheel; pops-up to keep an eye on the road; and inputs, him being tense: 'Righto! Basically you are tied with me in that sin, from the start! I think you have earned a share of fifty-fifty, and I mean in cash, plus desirable gold! Dan, is you not excited?'—Dan beams from a thrill; and taken silence, nods his head as if agreed; then he re-joins: 'Beyond doubt! Yet, what is going happen with us next?'—

Robert thinks for a bit; then, is fixed his eyes on the road.

A sudden Rob's mood alters, as he turns jumpy and gloomy; as summits to Dan: 'But Swift won't get the gold and cash from me, no way! Since we want cash for us only, need a plan, partner?'—

Later that night once arriving in his shack, after Robert has left the car outside, and without delay, is begun climbing up on that loft . . .

Up on loft via perceive familiar steps, bird opened its eyes; Gale at once flew out of Dollhouse that, Robert did build? Once magpie is landing down where it's resting on edging of roof's wooden peak.

The minute Robert enters loft's room, where at once clarifies to Gale, like bird was waiting for him. He then drops a sack down on the floor; and began telling magpie, as touching upon troubles. He talks be rim, but amused: 'So, Gale you have done a good job today! And deserve an award for premium! It is night now anyway, but tomorrow I will get you something exotic to eat! How it's sound, Gale?'—

Ensuing he spins to observe the site, like so he is seeking place to hide the sack? On opposite side, seeing as magpie sways with its wings, takes off up and around; next Gale is landing down on Robert's upper arm. There is hearing an echo of the crow's cry. On the spot Rob's mind be disrupted, while is breathing deeply; he then assumed: 'Where can I hide the goods? What if Cops tomorrow start interrogating? I have to take care of . . .'—

Chapter 20

It's a beautiful morning in Macau. Saw Robert has arrived in a taxi, and debarked. He is carrying suitcases, when is walking through to the Marina; and entering into the Ferry terminal. Robert stops in a flash; looks around, be caution. On the spot he is begun seeking an aimed metal box . . .

Soon Dan that is carrying a huge container too embarks on. Henceforth, he has joined Robert in . . .

On the outside meanwhile, at the Ferry Terminal, came across a ferryboat with first travelers aboard that cast off from the Harbor.

. . . On thus tension Dan is tense, when talks: 'I told you everything would be okay? Didn't I?'—He then looks around tensely, but has felt sleepy. Robert on the other hand yawns, and rubs his eyes: 'If you say-so? Dan, do you think we can make a good deal with those local folks to sell bullion?'—Dan in its place is cheery: 'I hope so, Kent?'—Rob too picks up jolly mood, let's hope we will go to make 'it back, before daytime?'—Dan agrees with him, is nodded his head: 'Upon our return you hang around harbor, while I will go to sleep?'—

Curtly the two nomads are in a boat, cruising of mix-up into a fog . . .

A minute ago, Rob arrived at Ferry Terminal, before Daytime, saw is content, likely trade went well.

After Rob walks through the sliding doors toward the storage lockers, whereas he seeks digits. Once he has found that aimed box on upper tear, saw next as Robert inserts coins within. Following he places inside a case that is covered with broadsheet. First Robert scrutiny, then he dials combination lock of that box. While he browses warily, and closes access. Henceforth Robert dials a number on his cell phone; and waits for someone to answer it. His voice is firm on the mobile, as he began talking:

'Hello, am I talking with Mister Swift?'—

Period in between in the condo: hear Swift's voice on the phone is a sleepy: 'Yes, this is he! Who is it?'—Robert on other side of the line talks into the phone is sarcastic: 'It's Wally from the Casino! Remember me, Swift?'—Swift next began talking into the phone: 'Ah, Wally or suchlike your name? How's our mutual business going?'—Robert listens warily; and is breathing. When next he is responding as it's faking: 'Fine! Nice to hear from you too, Ron?'—Swift on other side of the line breathing, he also is listened. Next man reacts, as his voice is in essence impatient. Ron is talking on the phone, aggressively: 'For your own sake! I did not doubt that you could! But tell me all about it?'—Robert on the phone line listens; but bears down on, and is spoken: 'Well, yesterday I worked as usual on the night shift. The whole thing progress smoothly; with no troubles . . .'—Soon after, Robert walks outside, in the harbor. He then stops; takes breathes; and prolongs telling: 'But I have to warn you, Mister Swift! From there I was managing to get only a velvet box, and cash . . .'—

Sudden Swift's voices prevent Rob from talking, as he is reacting by gnashing your teeth; when began yelling into the phone: 'We have made a deal? I told clear and simple for you must bring me gold plus the cash from there! What you're a retard?'—The two on both sides of the lines listen warily, while is breathing into the phone-sets. Resultant Swift is prolonged, and talks in a firm voice: 'Wally, listen carefully if you wish I can call Interpol or in our Police, and tell there about you're . . .'—Swift stops short; takes breaths, like restraint himself; he then snaps: 'Also for you're not getting bored in the services, I also reveal about your mate to throw there! Are you guessing, which one I mean?'—Robert listens carefully what Swift tells on other side of the line. He shakes his muscles; breathes in; says-so is daring: 'Mister Swift, I warn you: neither to daunt me, nor talk in such tone! When I have got there, where directly I was heard someone's steps! So, I have picked up that box with some cash, and left without delay!'—Hear both on their phone lines are breathing intensely; at the same time as they listen warily to each-other. Robert then shakes his head, and prolongs of yarn into the cell phone; it saw he is sly, with a smirk: 'Ron I have covered my ass not to be caught? I even can tell you more, as Confucius has said: "He was being caught red—handed!" It's no way I would live in fear, Ron! Because I plan working in this 'Casino! Does it make sense to you?'—Those two on their phone lines are breathing in silence, and having thought. Swift tells more in an odd intonation: 'I follow, you're! But you know what, Wally, you have let me down! I thought you are an expert? But you have acted like a cat burglar!'—Rob on the phone line browses; is amused. He then enlightens, and says-so being ironic: 'Fine cheery up, Ronald MacDonald!'—Robert stops short; takes gulps of air; and prolongs telling him over the phone: 'Listen to me. I am in the Harbor right now. I have put a velvet box and cash in the case, which to be found in a locker six of the box with digit sixty-six. You will get the box from the locker. Simultaneously you have to call my friend. Do you grasp, Ron?'—In a critical point Robert is gasping for air, while he looks through. Still, the two on both sides of lines are breathing into their phones. Now Robert talks in a calm voice: 'I told you, where the goods to be located? Come here any time, Ron and get from the box 66!'—Those two on both sides of the phone lines are panting anxiously, and listen carefully.

Robert first is prolonged, in a tense voice: 'Do you need a box, Ron or you want to put me in jail? What do you want?'—Swift stops Rob, is deceitful; and his voice by fret; when alone began talking: 'Enough of extreme! I need some time. As Confucius once has said: "The cautious seldom errs!" As you have said, it's a good idea for anyone not to see us together, Wally?'—Those two on both lines are breathing. Swift then starts yelling in a hostile voice about Rob's involvement in incident; and he is incessant: 'Then again, it opts if you cashed in from that safe? If I do find out that you're a liar, and have redeemed riches; but played me alone? I will hunt you down, even if it takes me to get my hands dirty!'—

After ending the phone argument; Robert remains in the harbor, is carefree; as his voice is with joy:

'Up yours! Catch me if you dare, Swift? . . .'—

Chapter 21

Robert is walking through the Center, when he came within reach of a 'Car Trade Shop', there saw be wholesale full of vehicles. He checks one-second handcar, when looks closely on it, which he is able to choose from . . .

Later views a taxi drove, and stops near car shop. See next Dan gets out of the car that, is holding a plastic bag with a set of beer kept in there.

Fifteen minutes later, Robert and Dan are in the parking lot, where both seated interior of a car that Robert has bought earlier.

Herein those two are listening to music on the car-radio that played in there. Now and there, Dan gave the impression of being excited: 'We just hit the jack pot!'—Dan nods his head, seen as he motions with his eyebrows.

Seen Robert is a bit intoxicated from sipping beer: 'Dan, do you know the meaning of a Cash Cow?'—Dan moves he's head up and down; and puts a smile; but still him being silent. Now Robert continual being cheerful: 'Well, I am happy to inform you instead of Cash Cow we have anew, as it's better than the old say Cash Crow!'—Dan at once began laughing; and in tandem ducks his head, whilst sees to, and looks be excited: 'Now, Rob you need anew ID and visa! A rumor has it someone does that for cash . . .'—

Hearing the news they are inhaling, and into their thoughts. While Robert nods his head up and down: 'You're right! How long it will take to get it done?'—Dan raises a hand up; then places behind on his neckline, and rubs it: 'We should go and see to it. I think it will take roughly a week to do it?'—

Chapter 22

Freshly daylight in Macau's Centre sees Robert under your own steam beside Dan, as they just have exited the 'Travel Agency', and both are blissful. Dan is eager to speak: 'I didn't expect this would take that long to get visas done? An ID was for you Rob, as well? Is that not a great idea Lee has done for us?'—Robert bows his head, but is tense: 'Yeah! As the old say by people: "money talks and bullshit walks"! Now call me Kent! Do business with Swift in no way will be grown! Let's hurry up to checkpoint, partner?'—

It's a fine daylight. Before now the double act were out of Macau, while now they advanced to Zhuhai Checkpoint. Seen both are seated in the interior of a car, and Dan is driving. From the time when they left, and by now they have come within reach of the Zhuhai Gongbei Checkpoint . . .

Meanwhile, one of the security guards is asked this duo to stop their car, so as them to join a long procession among other folks in the queue? Saw Robert is worried, like so he whispered: 'Okay. Pray that, officers don't find money in our car?'—Dan too is panicky, when has a word: 'You just keep cool, and silent? I will do the talking here, Okay?'—Rob barely nods his head like agrees; still he is felt panic-stricken.

It's a longtime pass. At present it's nightfall. Though this duo not far-off Macau, but climate here is affectedly changed tropics to cold.

This duo stood in line, yet being waiting of fret for their visas to be processed . . .

When next Robert glances through; but he is tense: 'We have waited a long time in the line?'—

Dan bows his head up and down: 'I know.'—Now they are given harmonized nods; still both appearing are worried?

Later that night to all appearances this double act has stuck in the China's Zhuhai Checkpoint, who knows for how long?

At long last, came the duo's turn to pass through the Gongbei Checkpoint with the purpose of getting into Zhuhai that be located on China's mainland. Soon hear the first officer talks in Cantonese: 'Mister Kent, what is reason for you're two coming in Zhuhai?'—Rob looks in this man's eyes, and responds:

'Our trip to China is strictly business!'—

It is ensuing a second officer intrudes, and in that case, stated: 'We have tariff among principles, but the whole thing be written in Chinese?'—Now Rob so-called Kent, intruded: 'This man is my partner, and he can translate for us!'—

On the spot a second Chinese official is scanning in detail the duo's IDS and visas. By the duo next deed, they are offering an official a deal seen: Money Change hands between these parties.

CHAPTER 23

Vision of a lovely dawn at China's Mainland, in Shenzhen. Even if the climate is felt frosty and smoggy, but it's sunshiny, bluish sky.

Now and there Rob is under a false name Kent that, by courtesy bows his head.

Given that next Robert, Kent, offer a business deal to a Chinese man Thong Wah is created wooden boats:

'Mister Thong, here is my share of the investment pro our mutual productions? . . .'—

Before now Robert was doing business with the man, Thong Wah: here money changed hand between them . . . Gladly Thong has offered Rob employment working as with the woodwork. For Robert is called Kent, all strange too many to him: awed how the Chinese men having created boats, made of timber.

Time in between, Kent is growing his business, by which his task to try it.

And before Rob knew it, he was begun crafting these Chinese style ferryboats.

CHAPTER 24

'Now is a year since Robert and Dan were fugitives. He has a new identity, Kent, for as long as it's safe for him. Robert dreams of the day, when he will return to US, and could get even with Martin, Cyclops; this one has ruined his life, and separated him from Nora. Yet he is willing to stay put, and wait for the right time to return home.' Meanwhile, Rob has settled at China's mainland in Shenzhen. Be under a false name Kent, he was enduring there with a career in Thong's workshop, whereas he has begun crafting ferryboats.

CHAPTER 25

One of those days Dan arrives at Rob be Kent's tool shed, where he still builds boats, which with luck . . .

Now and there, Ming waits for a while until Robert is called Kent, lunchtime break come to pass.

Soon after, came into the view those workforces are having lunch, and eating Chinese famous dishes . . .

Period in between, Dan is discussing with Robert about their living, he looks cheery, and slaps his arm: 'I have not seen you for a while. How are doing, buddy?'—Robert puts a wide smile; then he's responded pompously, but he watches, as murmurs: 'So far so good! I am utterly keen on working here with woods!'—Dan is leering; and nods with his head: 'I was ignorant that, you are skilled in joinery, Kent?'—On impulse Rob's upper arms began shaken: 'Well, my friend, now you do! Soon the Dragon Boat Festival is coming . . . And mister Thong gave orders for we are to start building boats from this time on. That creation Thong relocates with those products to the Chinese seaports, and sent to other provinces?'—Robert is Kent stops short; taken gulps of air; he seems being at a complete loss. Dan puts a smile, and spoke his opinion: 'Kent, you're very shrewd?'—

But Robert, doesn't hear him, and remains in that strength of mind, for a while . . .

. . . Suddenly Robert's mood alters to gloomy: 'All is good! But I deeply miss my family, and Eleanor most of all?'—In that case Dan slants his head on sign:

'Then, why don't give them a call, Kent . . . ?'—

For the time being, Robert sits in the subsidiary workshop, where he has lost track of time . . .

Sudden memories bring to Robert's mind, and he has found himself back in the family home. There he is without problems shed light on his phishing scams . . .

Later Robert dials a number on his cell phone; and waits anxiously to hear a familiar voice on other side of the telephone line to respond.

Meanwhile in Lipinski's house is night: where heard the phone buzz. Rosalyn answers the call, and her voice on the phone by hums: 'Hello, Rosalyn's speaking!' Robert of the phone line was breathless. On a critical point Rob is panting on the phone; he then barges in: 'Hi, mom! It's me, Robert! I am alive . . .'—On a whim, the two on both sides of the lines are struggling for breath; while listen to each-other. Rosalyn is distressed to cry with bliss, when she talks, and her voice shaky on the phone: 'Are you truly my son Robert?'—Where on other side of the line, in a subsidiary shed Robert laughs; and reacts without delay: 'Yes, mom, it's really me Rob! I am alive, and speaking to you!'—In residence, on other side of the line Rosalyn is weeping, and is wheezing, then she answers: 'My sweet Robert! All this time I felt that you are alive? Hugo didn't believe that you died!'—She calms down a bit nods her head, is full of joy: 'Robert, where are you now? When can you come home? Oh, my God! I forgot police was after you, son?'—Back in the shed: Robert's courtesy, as is agreeing with her, still kept calm, but his voice gloomy on the phone: 'Mom, I can't come home! Not yet! You know why! Mom, do not tempt me?'—There those two on both sides of the phone line silently; and they are also listening. Rosalyn talks, in a calm voice: 'I know son, it's important here for your safety! I want what is best for you, my son! Robert, let me tell you a piece of good news for a change . . . ?'—In shed Rob; listens to her voice, be intrigued; but edgy. A sudden he stops her: 'How is everyone at home, tell me? What's Nora doing, how is she?'—Saw Rosalyn is keen: 'Don't worry about it we all well! Son, I just want to tell you the latest news . . .'—

CHAPTER 26

The next morning, be in Interpol's office, in the US, whereas view Colubrine is sitting around the table. Sees he's talking over the telephone with someone; hearing his voice is a commanding:

'What did you say? You're assured about that? . . .'—

Once inspector has ended phone conversation, when plunges into a chair, then he's into own thoughts.

A sudden self-wide opens the door; as is looking through gaps in. This is Martin that grins; and nods with his head: 'Inspector, can I come in?'—Colubrine angles his head, facing Martin; gestures at him. He then raises his eyebrows up: 'Yeah. What is it McDermott?'—Martin looks excited, and swiftly is seat down opposite to chief. It follows that he shows up him through gestures: 'Yesterday our boys have traced a phone call to the Lipinski house!'—Colubrine looks oddly, wide-open eyes at Martin; as is matching too inspector shuddering with his upper-body. Now Colubrine bows head as be busy: 'What is so strange about that call?'—Martin folds up his hands: 'Inspector, don't you want to know, who's called there?'—Colubrine tongue in cheek: 'And, who would this be? A Ghost from the shop?'—Martin leers; and talks boldly: 'You may say that! This is about a ghost! Cause Rob Lipinski called home, this Son of a Bitch is alive!'—Colubrine heeds, a look at Martin, like saw a ghost, and by inquisitive look is assumed of fret: 'You're definite the call was from him?'—Martin nods, as if is self-assured: 'No doubts, chief!'—Colubrine on a critical point bows his head down, and has said in vulgar: 'Oh, fuck me!'—Martin is sustained eagerly: 'I have listened, and recognized Rob's voice on tape! He has also told Rosalyn that, want Nora to fly in Hong Kong . . . ?'—

. . . Colubrine quickly dials a phone number suchlike; and began talking with someone and to anywhere. He in talks a tense voice on the phone: 'Hi, Captain! We need your help? My team and I are flying to Hong 'Kong so as to arrest someone in your country? . . . '-Once Colubrine ends the phone talk, he then presses switchboard, and gave the officers a command. He turns aside is facing Martin. Colubrine appears be amazed, and tells like so: 'Great job! Life is a miracle? Associate of mine there clued-up us to man named Ming, who's opened an account over there?'—He discontinues. Martin nods his head, be subdued. Colubrine extends: 'Pack your stuff, Martin, as we will embark on Hong Kong!'—

Chapter 27

A view of a radiant cock-crow in Hong-Kong.
Somewhere in the apartment building is a vision: in a wide bathtub hearing splashes around. Inside the room is foggy. There through a glass-sill could be seen two silhouettes they are Robert and Nora. Yet a vision is fuzzy, where they are kissing there in. Developing into them is begun lovemaking . . .

A tad later those two lovebirds are out of the wash; Nora enters lounge room, is wearing a robe over that covered her body. As Rob sees her and alters shyly; and budges with his upper-body . . .

Soon those put heads together. Nora beams, and is fond of happiness that has returned to her; and it's shared by both of them . . . View Robert's look, fortuity reflected in his eyes.

Eleanor is with a stare at him lovingly: 'Rob, what is it?'—In that case Robert spins; his face is glowing: 'Nora, I still can't believe that we are together again?'—Nora is glowing; and nods her head: 'Me too, darling? I haven't got any hopes to see you alive? That felt you're!'—Robert takes breaths; gave a nervy grin; and he declares, while shakes his head:

'I know how you feel? Then and there it wasn't my choice! I love you Nora! You can't even imagine how long I make-believe for this day to come?'—He breathes; he is drawn near Nora, and held her hand in his. Following he is kissing her passionately . . .

Some minutes later he began talking again: 'I don't want to worry you? But, I am afraid we have to flee again?'—Hearing the news, Nora turns pale as be of fret, and starts talking at once. Still be edgy she said nicely: 'Get away? Why? Where's to?'

Rob stops Nora; and began stroking her, ensuing by kissing her hair; is sincere and gently: 'Shush . . . There you're. I will get you a permit! You have to get to the Bank, in Hong Kong?'—He stops looks at her, as if trusting her with a secret, when he murmurs, is tense: 'In Bank make a deposit, there you need to exchange money into Hong-Kong 'Dollars, which must hide in a sack? We then will meet at someplace, and leave jointly for . . .'—

Chapter 28

It's nightfall in Kong Hong, where be seen a full moon excel outwardly, up in the atmosphere.

Meanwhile, in downtown's restaurant saw Rob sits beside Nora around the table. Those lovebirds' are amused, having a good time there. Nora has worn chic clothes, where of her left hand ring finger is a band. Rob's well-dressed; gain upon his hand tied on a gold wristwatch. This pair is looking in each-other's eyes that, reflected them being in love.

Soon a recognizable waiter came within reach of them, he's well mannered drawn near this match pair up, and is asking over: 'Good evening, Mister Kent! What would like to order?'—Robert inclines to Nora, as they are whispering and beam to each-other.

Rob raises his head, looks at a waiter; briefings him, as nods his head: 'Yes, we want champagne with caviar . . .'—

. . . Once this waiter leaves; it seems Eleanor be stunned. On a whim be intrigued by, she asked: 'Robert you're amazed me? By the way, I know him? Isn't Dan your friend?'—Robert moans of a warning to her; as is to shut her up: 'Shush. Uh-ah! Think before you say it?'—Yet, Nora feels tense: 'Robert, where have you got a great deal of cash, all the time?'—Rob bows head down, as he pulls up looks in her eyes. By way of joy he is glowing: 'Stop it! I feel it's amazing! We're together at last! You're my wife and I love you! Don't you love me? Key to happiness in a way lay is we must have faith in one-another!'—Nora looks lovingly at him; when draws near; takes his hand in hers, she began whispering; is shy: 'Of course I love you!'—When Eleanor began talking, her voice being fluctuated with frets. It looks like she is begging him: 'Robert, I am scared for you, and I don't want to lose you again! What if someone finds out that three of us will be staying here?'—Nora saw in his possessions a huge amount of cash; she utters be fretful: 'What's that?'—And Rob's reaction is: 'Dan and I are careful, don't worry!'—But Eleanor wouldn't stop: 'Do you on loan to someone? I do not like to repay, as be harassed? What if creditors demand a big payout?'—Robert takes Nora's hands kiss them; then raises his head up, and looks into her eyes: 'Do I look that I have borrowed cash from creditors? Or do you think I will do something to jeopardize all of us?'—She lures charmingly: 'Okay, if you say-so? Let us have a great time tonight, darling?'— Nora is glowing, like is trying to seduce him tonight.

PART III

CHAPTER 29

In Hong Kong's suburbs on a warm night, where Robert subsidiary workshop is situated, where seen he be seated at the table, and does a consumption.

A sudden magpie is flown in; and it lands on window surface. View the bird jerks its tiny head down that is meant rather?'—Robert seems is dazed by bird's activity: 'Gale, is that something you want 'me to do?'—Next came magpie's response: 'Kar!'—But Gale saw it doesn't sink to Rob of her aim; then magpie uses a beak; and is begun ripping off a teeny-tiny bag that made of aluminum, down from its mini neck . . .

Robert appears be shocked: 'Gale, you want me to remove the bag?'—Here saw the magpie is in motion.

On the Spot Robert seemingly is intrigued by Gale activities; so he takes in. His upper-body leans onward: 'Why, do you want to take off the bag? It's terribly phishing is going to happen?'—

CHAPTER 30

It's sunlight hours, in Hong Kong. Saw Nora is under your own steam, in the direction of the Bank located at downtown, roughly for fifteen minutes . . .

At last Nora comes close to an aimed Bank. After she glances through, then without a care in the world Nora goes into the Bank, and carrying along a dark sack on her back. She is under pressure, as mumbling to herself: 'Where's the entry? I hope no one saw me?'—She stops, is warily; glances around; and bows her head; Nora then steps into the Bank.

At that day and time, a group of people is remained in the Airport's Customs, whereas those was having disembarked from a plane; and waiting for their turn to get through check-in. See they are wearing suits, among whom came into sight Colubrine beside is Martin stood apart, as they having arrived in Hong Kong.

Here at the airport beside those men in suits that are pushing into Airport Security for their stuff to be checked as the priority.

Saw amid them Martin is mobile in back that group.

Colubrine looks around a new place, he then spins, and attend to: 'Martin, we came here at last! Let's go now quickly, in search for those fugitives?'—

Martin and the rest of that bunch are nodding with their heads in agreement. Its already night entered. For the time being, saw in Federal office Martin sits beside Colubrine with other officials that bend down, and is looking into the computer monitor seeking of someone?'—

Soon Colubrine rises up close to VDT: 'So, lad do you have something for us yet?'—First policeman spins; lifts his head up, and is assuming: 'Nothing new, inspector!'—On a whim, Colubrine hits desk's edging: 'Goddamn! How could it be?'— Again he hits over a desk edging: 'Try in one go searching all the Banks? Allow web go around the world . . . ?'—

Quite time passes in Hong-Kong's Federal office. Now it's time after mid-night, where in the Police HQ being observed Colubrine, who bends down over one of the officer's, that seems, is engaged on the computer.

Sees a second officer bow his head down with a stare on VDT; he then suddenly yells: 'I found something, inspector! Yesterday, someone by a name of Nora Lipinski had deposited a sum of $5 millions, roughly, which in Hong Kong Dollars?'—Martin deeds are of fanatical, when he endorsed: 'Go ahead, and track her address, my friend?'—

CHAPTER 31

A view is a red-blood crack of dawn in Hong Kong. Exterior of the workshop, where Robert was employed in saw glimpse of light be on, this gave indication that someone is inside?

From nowhere chain of the police cars drove and are arriving in Robert-Kent subsidiary workshop . . .

A minute ago the police force an entry into that workshop; in quirk of fate no one be found, given it was empty inside.

On a critical point Martin looks be gloomy, when he has said: 'How could that be? Where are they?'—

On the spot they are hearing noises, as one is in motion. That team runs directly to the place.

In the next room came into view Dan, who in a difficult situation has tried to escape them, but be caught in clash with the Chinese police and Interpol. Now the first officer yells in Cantonese: 'Go, get him, guys!'—

A minute ago Dan is out of his depth, when got in a clash with that force, throwing punches from side-to-side towards few, but one at the time, where he stood in back.

Sideways saw anew Copper began yelling in English:

'Where is your cohort Lipinski, with his phishing scam wife?'—Sees Dan is rebellion: 'I don't know what you're talking about? And, I am not acquainted with this name? You have got all wrong! My name is Tang Wah . . .'—

Spur-of-the-moment Colubrine stops Dan; he is grim, and spoke: 'Don't play dumb with us? Yeah, Tang my ass! I know damn well you're Ming, and Lipinski is your partner in crimes!'—

In a difficult situation Dan's begun thrown punches at one of the officers. Rashly he jumps with determination; at the same time moves back and forth on a salto, as stood up-front. On a critical point he manages escape across glass-sill; he is resulting to hurdle upon the open-air. Hear Colubrine badges in: 'Guys, follow him! Don't let him slip away? He can bring us to Lipinski!'—

Police is following, and searching for Robert. one officer resultant shakes his head, and is assumed. A first officer urgently says to Colubrine: 'Inspector I think they have gone by the sea?'—

An officer then turns, and points to the window: 'The way for them to move around is by boats!'—

CHAPTER 32

At the same day at late morning, in the Harbor saw Dan, Nora and Robert send-off on ferry that, belong to someone, as they are traveling on high-speed . . .

Observation is zero across the marine, be caused by fog that overshadows a view of the Sea . . .

Given Dan is running toward a pier; by made a stop on the way, he then spins to sideways and is watching at afar; but him being on edge.

On a critical point Dan is breathing; talks tensely: 'Kent and you're Nora, get quickly in the boat. And, let castoff . . . !'—But Kent stops him short, be curious: 'Dan, what is going on?'—

Dan instantly turns to look around, and saw he is on edge, when responded: 'The local police with Cyclops in back are coming after us?'—

At sunrise two boats with first travelers aboard a Chinese ferry, have sendoff outward the Harbor.

There this trio boarded a ferry, and by now is on crossing that cruising of mix-up into a fog . . .

Still at daylight hours, seen one of ferry's reeled faster, where this trio's ferry is tagging behind.

A tad later the skipper from a second ferry came in close proximity to Robert's vessel. Hear a skipper talks to that crew. And next a chat started between him and Robert-Kent: 'Here is the boat that can win a race?'—

In a boat that crew agreed with Leader as one, and gave nod of their head. On the spot came Kent's retort: 'Yes, boss! It's time catch fishy?'—Skipper gave a smile; and nods his head; signs to go on, then ahead. A skipper then declares: 'You right! Don't forget it's the time for Dragon boat festival? Kent, you make us a

good boat next time?'—Robert looks at him; takes gulps of air;
and produced a nervy smile; when he is responded:

'Mister Thong, I don't know, yet? It depends what fate has 'in
store for me?'—

Shortly saw Thong navigates, and handles course of the boat;
by way of it has cut through the water . . .

Since Robert is on board a ferry that kept rolling, hereafter, a
sudden boat's propeller seems stopped working just now; which
has resulted been reducing boat's speed, in an attempt to avoid
a disaster . . . From air tides rise up, given that Robert's boat is
swaying back and forth on waves . . .

Crossing Dan does fix on becoming an oarsman, as he knows
how too. In the midst of the high Sea, Robert starts rowing as fast
as he is able, it's like two oarsmen could.

Fifteen minutes later this trio in the midst of the sea view
Eleanor short-term is breathless; so she takes a lot gulps of
air. Given the fact that she bends over board, and stares into
deep dark waters . . . . Still be bent over Eleanor looks into the

deep; a sudden swing of mood came over her to dull: 'Jesus, it's still dark and cool on alfresco? And, it is raining cats and dogs too . . .'—

. . . From nowhere the trio is sighted a motorboat spun cutting over the water, crossing to their spot. There they are caught in the midst of sea waves.

Unforeseen a crackdown on boat's speed, whereas the trio is gaining slowly its through their cruise.

Be caught unaware Robert is edgy, so he's yelling: 'Guys, be careful of high waves! . . .'—

. . . A few feet there on the Cop's speedboat, by which driver goes faster, where speedboat picks up over waves in an attempt to reach this trio's ferry.

Saw a risky situation, out of the blue a crow flew; and it is landing down on Martin's upper arm. Look-see Martin tries to get rid of an annoyed crow; and at once he spills out on it. He is like a cat on a hot tin roof: 'Fuck you crow! Where in hell it came from? I will kill you bloody crow . . . !'—

Seen a magpie sways with its wings; and flew away.

On the spot in the midst of the sea, aboard ferry a magpie soaring over the trio's heads. Then a crow is landing on boat's upper corps apex, where those three are awash.

Once Nora saw a crow, has become shaky; and so be her tone of voice: 'Where the crow came from? I am scared, Robert!'— Robert looks in front, puts a smile, and is reacting, together caressing Nora's hair, then he is saying: 'Don't be scared, Nora? It is Gale! The magpie can see far ahead in a fog?'

Later at one fell swoop in the midst of sea view the Police speedboat presses on gas; undertaken so as to reach Robert's boat . . .

Next one amid those police officers began shooting in a straight line toward Robert's ferryboat . . .

. . . Unexpectedly the speedboat comes within reach of Robert's vessel; as a result the officer blows away through that lower part of the ferryboat.

Resultant Robert turns aside; is edgy: 'It's a hog-wash? Cyclops is approaching us, look up? . . .'—

A sudden Rob's ferry starts rotating, then on the spot, it is capsized.

By way of those three have fallen overboard into the Sea . . .

Just relatively ten minutes have past; given that trio still swam deep in the waters . . .

At this juncture Martin bends over, reaches for the trio are in the water, so as to get them aboard the police speedboat . . .

Martin screams on top of his lung, eagerly: 'I have caught you at last, Son of a Bitch!'—

While Robert doesn't pay attention, in its place delays, saw his upper-body lean over to grab hold of Eleanor, who is a washed, its like he is to helping her out. Martin looks be abhor toward Robert: Your motherfucker, Lipinski! Do you thought that, could escape from us? No way!'

In a difficult situation, Robert is out of breath: 'Ah-ah, fuck me!'—It's resulting the police are helping first Eleanor, when she tugs up aboard. Dan next is pulled out is filled with water from top to toes. And, the last saw Robert that, be towed up. Up-to-the-minute that trio is surveys in chilly waters, where they are freezing from it . . .

See Nora, Dan and Rob are getting apiece of towels to dry up . . .

A sudden Martin's commanding voice is yelling: 'Now, Mister Ming and you Lipinski, kneel down! Do it! Put the hands behind your heads! You are all under arrest . . . !'—

Saw the trio self-conscious: raised heads up; but they look are worried. Dan stops Martin, is ironic: 'What's the hurry? We are not going anywhere?'—He points a hand all through: 'Don't you see, the Sea 'surrounds us all? No one can escape?'—On the spot Robert spins see to Nora; then turns back, and is facing Martin; while he looks and talks being disgust: 'Yep!'—On a whim Robert turns aside; thus he adds more, be ironic: 'Oh, Martin before I forget, you strike for me a chord of felon? I will gladly be going under the sea with Captain Nemo, just to escape your madness, Cyclops!'—

CHAPTER 33

At the same day it's a red-blood twilight. Here is brought to our attention Martin is in the car, and accelerating to an isolated site. On a critical point he's kept pressing on gas to go faster, like so he is chasing the Crow . . .

Later, apparently vehicles with the forces on board advanced, then they have driven downhill.

At some stage of trip Martin's car ascents. Given he is speeding up, and is driving like mad for the forestry, so that following a crow in-flight . . .

Given that vehicle drove for at least some miles, while aside in the Cop's cars has come in front of Martin's; and in a critical points his car then noisily breaks . . .

To view Martin's car speedometer has shown: 90 km, 95 km . . . 100 km . . . and it is kept climbing high . . .

Time in between saw the magpie is airborne. A sudden Gale comes clattering down, given that bird has by now, landed on top of tree's wide branch . . .

Those Cops in chased speedboat is matching a magpie that airborne over dry land . . .

Martin has driven on high-speed relatively for a time, as he is figured out of the magpie's trick that he tries to bring to a halt his car . . .

Without warning he is unable to cling to controls of the car's wheel . . .

Resulting on high speed Martin's car hit trunk of the same tree, where the magpie is seated up on it.

Causing by that profound thrash this tree is just about to crash, and slowly tumbled . . .

Given that magpie sways with its wings; and is on track flying away, on the spot . . .

In the twinkling of an eye magpie attempt to go up and fly, promptly Colubrine removes a gun from his holster, and is fired shots up at a soaring Crow . . .

In a difficult situation Robert yells on top of his lungs: 'No! Gale, no! Fly back! . . .'—

But it's too late: inspector has shot straight on target: spontaneously magpie began plummeting down. Caused by bullet that hit Gale, the magpie was tumbling to the ground . . .

Robert saw what Colubrine did; is shouting; but he became apprehensive: 'Oh, no! God . . . '-A breach between Robert's stand and squad of Cops.

Once Robert saw magpie clear-fell down, and without further ado, he is running toward the site, where Gale's carcass has been lying down . . .

In next to no time Robert came within an inch of the carcass to be found. Out of respect Rob goes down on his knees, like so is expression of his grief.

First Robert tries to revive magpie through strokes over its wings, and began shaking carcass of a dead magpie's beak . . . Repercussion

Follow-on Robert began singing to magpie, which has a special verse to be called upon. By way of sorrow he is sobbing; and says in slogan: 'Gale, come on open your eyes! You are my most loyal friend in the whole world!'—He keeps peace for sake of magpie memory: 'Oh, God, what I have done? Please, Gale don't die on me?'—

At that point Eleanor has advanced; and is begun caressing Robert's upper arm. At the same time she is distressed to cry, as says-so: 'Rob, what you're blaming yourself for? So what if a Crow is dead?

'Come on, let's go, darling?'—

Without turning his head up Rob is seated down on the ground, when he replied angrily: 'You don't know what you're saying? Better if you shut up, Nora!'—Rob ineptly says to a corpse: 'I am sorry Gale! You were devoted to me, more than any in this world?'—Hearing his comments, by which it hurt Eleanor, and she is begun crying. Impulsively she state, and is sobbing: 'Why did you say that? What about your family and me? Your mother, Hugo and I are all love you very much, Robert!' But Robert is firm; when in a warm voice warns her: 'Nora, I love my family and I love you're! Just as we speak, let me take care of my magpie Gale for the last time. Go, now! Leave me to be alone, please? . . .'—

Prior turning his back on her, Rob looks down at her purse, places his hand in, and withdraws from a scarf out. Next he spins, it seem is mad at Martin.

Meanwhile, the Cops are running toward site, where Martin is lying down on the ground. It's sited he is not far from a dead magpie, Gale, which does being positioned.

Without more ado Rob places a hand in his pocket.

Given the forces that are targeted Rob, and holding gun-barrel toward him. In a flash Rob has removed a hankie, then pullouts an army knife out of his pocket.

Next he lays a dead body of a magpie inside hankie, and gently folds all the angles down from cloth up, over it's belly, via making it into a triangle.

Given he is begun digging downward the soil that, resembled to a teeny-tiny graveyard . . .

A sudden one of the officer's yells in a commanding voice, and his echo that has scared Robert on the spot: 'Hey, Rob! What the devil you're doing down there? Why do you need a knife, for?'—

In spur-of-the-moment inspector stops the officer, and alone commands this man with nodding his head up and down: 'Hey officer, leave him alone! Let him do it! He wants to say goodbye to a partner' . . .—

Impulsively memories start flooding Robert's mind, as he is looking back of all those times he has spent since his childhood with the magpie, Gale . . .—

A few minutes later, down on the ground sees Martin some some yard off that beaten track. When by effort of the policemen he was removed from his ablaze back car windowsill.

Providing a temp medical help, Martin was put aside by one of the forces; saw him being severely injured, which has caused by that horrible car accident. In quirk of fate Colubrine and other policemen are unable to help Martin repercussion of his condition worsen by second, caused by flowing of blood from his wounds . . .

Thus inspector appears be gloomy: 'Hold on! Martin, Ambulance is on the way?'—In its place, Martin tries to put a smile: 'Inspector, you have killed two birds with one stone!'—

Robert beside Eleanor and Dan briefly are standing in silence; now they have come within reach of these crowds, with a guard that is walking in back.

Meanwhile, Martin aside glances at this trio, and tried to raise his head up. He is feeling weak. But Martin calls upon Robert to come closer, and alone murmurs; while is wheezing: 'Rob, could you come up here? I want to talk to you, in private?'—

In the meantime, sees Robert is gnashing your teeth, being hostile towards him; and on a critical point he postpones, as is tongue-tied, but tied restraining himself . . .

In split seconds Colubrine began pushing Rob that sways pretty much be unstable. Eventually Rob looms slowly toward

Martin's respite, and observes him. In its place Robert is in motion, given that Martin's breathing deepens. Rob has resultant, as bent down; and moved closer to view Martin's injure; hearing he is begun kindly mumbling: 'Rob, you must be angry with me?'—Robert is tense, and reacting tensely: 'What do you think, Martin?'—

Now Martin took a chance, is licked his lips about it, and saw to Rob: 'I know how you feel!'—

Next turning his head aside, Martin tackles one of the officer, while he is out of breath: 'Can I get some water to drink, dudes?'—

Here saw inspector has advanced that, kneels down, and is moving closer to Martin; gave a grin; he then talks kindly: 'How you're doing, McDermott? Do you feel pain?'—Martin yet grown to be bold to have a serious talk with him, during which silence is held between the parties, at the same time as licked his lips: 'No! You cannot have a drink!'—Now Martin is wheezing, when he's stated: 'Chief, I won't go to make it! My last appeal: Chief, just as we speak promise not to charge Rob Lipinski! It's all utterly my fault! Now, I am thirsty! Can you get me some water, please?'—Colubrine takes gulps of air; thence moves his head up and down, like he has agreed. Next inspector began talking kindly: 'Okay! I will see what I can do, partner?'—

Inspector directly moves aside so as to get a drink for him.

In quirk of fate Martin deals with Robert. His eyes are showing, when he looked into Rob's eyes, and allude: 'Listen to me, Lipinski . . .'—Even if Martin is out of breath, his upper-body leans toward him: 'I have received ghastly wounds, this way I won't survive! And, I don't have much time! Listen to me, Rob, for the reason that I wish to confess . . .'—In that case Robert bow his head down: 'Look, Martin, I don't know what to say . . . ?'—Given Martin is gloomy that, stopped him: 'Don't say a thing, just listen! I need to shed light on back then when you were working in the construction, it was my fault: it was I who cut the ropes. Sadly a worker was injured . . .'—Now Martin stops, seen he is wheezing, and his body being shaky: '. . . I want you to be blamed for that accident! Yet, you were bared . . .'—Martin rests a bit; sucks in air, except for him being struggling for oxygen . . .

Vision of Robert's face has altered to pale, while he has clutched his fists, as if being ready of hard-hitting Martin . . .

Only Martin destructs him, alone is prolonged with his story: '. . . Next my obsession with Nora? But she's being in love with you! And, yet I tried to get of rid you're . . .'—He takes a rest, as looks with plead into Rob's eyes; and stated: 'So, I am begging you are, Robert for forgiveness, and Eleanor too?'—

Just now Nora emerges accompanied by Colubrine; and gave the lowdown; but says in a gently voice: 'I am sorry too, Martin. Please, forgive me because I was unable having any feelings for you! My love was and eternally is, for Robert only!'—Now Martin is intruded; gave a nod, like so he's shown her to leave. Henceforth Martin tackles Rob, and is heartfelt; he then fixed his eyes on him: 'I realize this now.'—

Next he turns his gawk to Robert: 'Speaking of eternity I have caught you at last Lipinski, but it doesn't mean a Goddam think, now . . .'—He stops; takes breaths; sees Martin being agonizing.

Meantime, Robert tries to calm him down: 'It's okay stay still, Martin, but don't move! This have worsen your pain . . . ?'—Here Martin stops Rob short, being with a nervy grin: 'I know that you're caring man, Rob, that's why I am asking for your sympathy? Let us get joyful, Rob! Say that you and I are friends, now?'—

Robert keeps peace for a minute . . .

On a critical point he acts like is easygoing; seen his body bends down: 'Okay, then! Martin, I forgive you! But you hold on a little more, buddy? Don't slip away? Doctors on their way, and will be healing you're, soon . . . ?'—Martin cuts short Robert's talking, instead alone murmurs, have the sense of hearing him wheezing: 'You don't need to be kind to me! I know well that I deserve your revenge? I have wasted my life chasing after you all out of envy! I will pay for as it happens because I am a sinner!'— He stops short; as began coughing; as nosebleed is shown upon Martin's upper-body.

Given that Robert is worried about him, and in a difficult situation he began smooth Martin's lips: 'Stop talking its doggy, buddy . . . !'—Rob interrupted by Martin; who comes to confess more; as have shaken his head, like is changed man: 'Don't butt-in, mate? I have got limited time left! I always envied you! But all the time you were ahead of me . . . ?'—He still is breathless: 'Ohm . . .'

Both have abided silently; then Martin prolongs:

'Now I wish that you to look after Nora, and for your own benefits, Rob . . .'—Martin discontinues of talking; saw is breathless; he then looks with a shame at Robert, who instead, slaps Martin over his upper arm: 'Am sure I will, mate! You take it easy, don't talk too much! Righto Martin? You need to keep your strength so as to live on, pal?'—

Given Robert holds awkwardly Martin's head that is in motion, and points up his eyes to the sky. On the course for those two becoming friends at last, Martin puts a smile; and is constantly whispering. He has fixed emits of blood that, being resulted of his wound; but endures to struggle for breath Martin's whole body and voice are shaky: 'It's a miracle Rob that, you will live to tell the tale?'—

It's a strike. Martin's breathing deepens; and prolongs by mumbling, as he talks in slogan: 'What's made sense to me now is "A straw that broke the camel's back!" It's about me, let us laugh'—Robert cuts him short, and alone says kindly: 'Martin, don't say that I . . .'—At this time Martin stops him, of saying; as waves his hand up in the air; and put in the picture. In the face of agony, Martin puts a smile, whilst being in pain: 'Let me talk! As for me, it's too late to survive on! I guess we will meet in afterlife, buddy? . . .'—

Another strike: Martin signs for Robert to lay his head down on soil. Next Martin has fixed his eyes on Rob; gave a grin; he then turns ogle up to sky . . .

. . . Until grave takes over, Martin loses color; thence he befalls being lifeless . . .

Quite times have passed since Martin died . . .

At last, Robert starts talking, but he is sadden:

'Okeydokey, pal! I will see you in heaven, but much later, I am not rushing, yet . . .'—

Still be on that site Robert approached Eleanor that stood near Dan, as his eyes is wide-open off fear. On a critical point he is with a stare that has changed to stun. Robert turns next and glances to Nora, when his breathe exaggerate; he shakes his head, says sadly: 'Today is tough day for all of us. In quirk of fate we got through horrors, which have ensued! I lost two of my best friends? Gale was my most loyalist companion! . . .'—

A sudden Colubrine has loomed on Robert, and intruded; when is prudently advised; and he murmurs kindly: 'Do not stress yourself about this crow death, Lipinski! The bird loved you as if in Swan fidelity be characteristic! Lipinski, but you're as a human, just as a man?'—

Now Rob looks awkwardly, and is dreary: 'Martin was envious towards me, and hated me too?'—He stops, but is gasping for air: 'To cite about, which has caused Martin being so mad, as he was obsessed with Eleanor? God have Mercy! Although in the end I forgave him?'—Dan shuts Rob up at this point, alone gently: 'You did the right thing, buddy!'—

This time Nora interrupts Dan; with a big smile. When she is looking at Rob, and entails ardently: 'Yes! Honey, I am only begging you to be relaxed! Let's make a fresh start?'—Rob looks at her as if he regrets; but keen: 'Nora, you're right! I am sorry, how I acted earlier! Let us start over?'—

Before long sees Colubrine came within reach of this trio, when has avowed gently: 'A wise man said: "There's no better time than the present!" What's made sense that you're three can be sendoff!'—

Succeeding with Lady luck for them, Dan came closer to Rob, and whispers, once again intrudes, but he is edge: 'Rob, did you focus to discuss on my future?'—Like this Rob nods his head, and is given a wink: 'What do you think? Yep! Your problem has been solved, my friend!'—

By way of looking next at Nora, Robert chuckles; whilst moves his head up and down.

On a critical point this trio looks at one another, while they are appearing joyful. Robert is felt blessed, like fate played for him, and on happy note he's embraced Nora. Ensuing he gave a wink as a sign to Dan; puts a smile, and he talks in slogan: "Birds of a feather stick together!"—

Bearing in mind of they still is vulnerable; Dan given a smirk, and tips his head aside: 'Yep!'—

Next Dan is curved his neck to a limited-access to Highway, like gave a hint; as he is joking: 'Let us get the hell out, guys? Before the good inspector has changed his mind!'—Dan then angle his head, and gave winks intent for Colubrine.

Robert stood beside Nora, when is begun patting her shoulders; and gave her a hint: 'Let's go, then?'—

Its appear they are unspoken, and zeal to escape.

Resulting they are begun walking away. Following them is Dan, like so this trio will embrace anew day.

THE END